"Don't you have any fa… you out with the baby?"

"No." He didn't elaborate. This woman didn't need to hear his sob story, and he hated it when people felt sorry for him.

"Friends?"

"Not locally." His single buddy at the vineyard had helped him buy his retail space but wouldn't be of any help in this case. "Would you consider a deal where we help one another out?"

"What kind of deal?" she asked with narrowed eyes.

"I could pay you to be his nanny."

She motioned to the laptop and stack of papers on one end of the desk. "I do have a business to run."

"I understand. What about something short-term until I can find a nanny?" She was already so protective over the baby, if he could just get her to start, maybe she'd want to continue helping him for longer. "What about one week?"

"Do you want me to take care of your son or teach you *how* to take care of him?"

"Both?" He attempted one of his signature smiles— one that usually made women giggle or swoon— but this time, it failed to obtain the desired result. Her expression was more of an I'm-not-impressed look, but he couldn't give up now.

Dear Reader,

Welcome back to Oak Hollow, Texas! *Lessons in Fatherhood* is the fifth book in my Home to Oak Hollow series. I have had so much fun creating this fictional Texas Hill Country town and its loveable, fun and quirky characters.

When small-town kindergarten teacher Emma Blake finds a baby in her new neighbor's art gallery, a letter says it's his child, but this is a surprise to Nicholas Weller. He's never even held a baby. He makes a deal with his standoffish and reluctant neighbor Emma for a week of baby lessons. Emma is still mourning her husband and daughter, and won't risk her heart again, especially not for a cocky confirmed bachelor who exasperates her. But she can't resist helping him for the baby's sake. One week of frustrating but funny lessons turn into many weeks, and she discovers he's a really good guy hiding behind a protective attitude. While they are both falling in love with the baby, will they fall in love with one another and be exactly what the other one needs?

I hope you enjoy *Lessons in Fatherhood*, and that you'll visit Oak Hollow again when the sixth book in the series is released. I love hearing from readers, and you can find all my social media information at makennalee.com. As always, thank you for reading!

Best wishes,

Makenna Lee

Lessons in Fatherhood

MAKENNA LEE

HARLEQUIN
SPECIAL
EDITION

HARLEQUIN®
SPECIAL
EDITION™

Recycling programs
for this product may
not exist in your area.

ISBN-13: 978-1-335-72409-0

Lessons in Fatherhood

Harlequin Enterprises ULC
22 Adelaide St. West, 41st Floor
Toronto, Ontario M5H 4E3, Canada
www.Harlequin.com

Printed in U.S.A.

Makenna Lee is an award-winning romance author living in the Texas Hill Country with her real-life hero and their two children. Her writing journey began when she mentioned all her story ideas and her husband asked why she wasn't writing them down. The next day, she bought a laptop, started her first book and knew she'd found her passion. Makenna is often drinking coffee while writing, reading or plotting a new story. Her wish is to write books that touch your heart, making you feel, think and dream.

Books by Makenna Lee

Harlequin Special Edition

Home to Oak Hollow

The Sheriff's Star
In the Key of Family
A Child's Christmas Wish
A Marriage of Benefits

Visit the Author Profile page
at Harlequin.com for more titles.

To my daughter, the baby girl I never got to know but will forever love.

Chapter One

I'm unplugging my alarm for a week. At the very least.

Kindergarten teacher Emma Blake wanted to sing and skip like she did with her class, but doing so while crossing the center park of Oak Hollow town square all alone might gain her a few sideways stares. But no one could stop her from dancing like a Rockette on the inside. Her students were adorable, but she'd been counting the days—and minutes—until summer break. Thankfully for all involved, it had been an early-dismissal day.

A warm gust of wind fluttered the full skirt of her Crayola-print shirtwaist dress and carried the delicious scent of freshly baked bread from the Acorn Café, reminding her she'd skipped lunch. It was hot like every other June day in Texas, but the sky was blue and next week's plan was set. Sleeping late, reading good books, spending time at her vintage shop and taking care of no one but herself. Heated from her walk, she twisted her long hair into a bun and secured it with a hairband.

Emma walked around the gazebo and studied their new sign from a distance. *Emma's Vintage & Creations by Jenny.* She once again had to control her urge to skip. The combination of Jenny's one-of-a-kind designs and her own vintage finds were working well together and bringing in new customers, and hopefully soon they'd have their online business up and running.

Just as she neared her shop, Nicholas Weller rushed out of the space next door. The space she and Jenny McKnight had wanted to buy for expansion, until this player from the city swooped into town and outbid them. His self-important attitude at the Oak Hollow business owners meeting had been a tip-off of what to expect. He'd introduced himself with the haughtiness of someone used to wearing tuxedoes and sipping expensive champagne while being served by his butler. When he'd told her to call him by his first name while straightening his designer tie, as if he was doing her a favor by allowing such casualness, she'd barely resisted an eye roll.

And now, in clothes too formal for a summer afternoon, Nicholas winked and grinned with his perfectly straight, white teeth as if she should fall at his feet and adore him.

Not happening, buddy. And who winks anymore?

Resisting a scowl—because her parents raised her right—she nodded politely.

Now they would have to listen to the construction noises as he remodeled with intentions of turning the old hat shop into an art gallery. It was unlikely such a place would make it in this Texas Hill Country town, but at least the space would be remodeled when he'd had enough of small-town life and decided to sell. He probably wanted to turn it into some ultramodern white space with chrome and glass, but thankfully the historical society wouldn't allow him to get rid of all the historic charm of the space.

This man with his two-seater sports car—which was taking up two parking spots—was so not her type.

She continued inside the shop her late grandmother built. "Hi, Jenny. How's business been today?"

"Pretty good." Little rainbows danced off the jeweled antique broaches in the velvet-lined tray Jenny adjusted on the counter. "A group of women who came in from San Antonio posted on social media saying this is their new favorite shop."

"Excellent. Can't go wrong with free advertising."

"How does it feel to be out of school for the summer?"

"Like I've won the lottery. I need a long rest followed by catching up on some Netflix series and staying up as late as I want. Probably while sipping an adult beverage and eating the junk food I've been denying myself." She put her tote bag under the register beside the little tea set and storybooks they kept handy for when Jenny's little girl visited the shop. "But don't worry. I'll still be here to help you every afternoon. And mornings, too, if needed."

Jenny's long, dark hair fell over her shoulder as she bent to straighten a pair of shoes. "Take a few days just for yourself. You deserve it. I can handle things here for the next few days because we have another new employee. I called the college student we decided on after interviews, and she was thrilled to accept the summer job. She starts tomorrow."

"Wonderful. I might take you up on that," Emma said, enjoying the sensation of her tension melting away. "But I'll probably end up at least stopping by every day."

"I brought a new dress I finished last night. It's a wrap style so it will fit a wider range of sizes." Jenny lifted a red-and-white dress from the rack beside her.

"Oh, wow. That's gorgeous. Let's put it in the window." Emma undressed one of the wireframe mannequins and fell into her favorite stress-reducing task of window dressing.

"If it sells quickly, I'll make more," Jenny said and handed her a red tulle petticoat.

"You should get started. I think it will be a hot seller. And I want one for myself."

"I've already started one for you," Jenny said. "It's turquoise."

"Perfect. You know me so well." Emma slid the petticoat underneath the full skirt to show off the huge red flowers on a white background, leaving a bit of the tulle peeking out along the hemline.

The string of silver bells above the door cheerfully jingled as customers came inside. They both welcomed the women and Jenny went to help them.

Over their soft mix of music dating back to the 1950s, she could hear a baby crying. Emma couldn't see anyone out the display window overlooking the square, and she'd swear the noise was coming from Nicholas's space next door. She put her ear to the shared wall and the sound grew louder. When the crying didn't stop, and there were no adult voices, her curiosity turned to concern. She had seen Nicholas leave but had not seen him return or anyone else go in.

Out on the sidewalk, she peered through his front plate-glass window. "Are you kidding me?" A diaper bag and car seat with an infant sat in the center of the mostly empty room. Had this man really left his child all alone? As if she needed another reason to dislike him. She tested his front door and it opened.

"Hello, is anyone here?"

With no answer, she crossed the room and kneeled beside the baby, but called out a few more times. Tiny pink feet had kicked free of the blanket and quivered with his cries. He was dressed in a green onesie covered with trucks and cars, so she assumed he was a boy and guessed that he couldn't be more than a few months old. Unable to stand the pleading cries, she unbuckled the infant from his carrier.

"There, there sweetie. It's okay." Cradling him close, she swayed and swaddled his feet in the soft blanket. The sight of a rabbit embroidered on one corner of the blanket made her breath stutter. The rapid beating of her heart matched the baby's, and she could almost hear Steven's voice calling her Bunny Rabbit. The baby stopped crying and blinked big brown eyes, his little mouth rooting against her. Emma nudged his tiny fist toward his mouth, hoping to temporarily pacify him.

So tiny. So precious. So brand-new and magical, still carrying that enchanting newborn quality as if brushed by angel wings. Longing to feed him from her own breasts, she felt her eyes prick with the familiar sting of tears. It had been more than three years, but flashes of pain still cut deep every time she thought about the accident that devastated her world.

"You are beautiful and precious, and *someone* shouldn't have left you alone."

Something banged in the back of the shop, and

her heart jumped into her throat. It sounded like a door had been flung open too hard.

"Is anyone back there? Mr. Weller?" She walked around a stack of boxes and down the short hallway to the office, which was also empty. But the back door was wide open. A chill shot through her, and she glanced into the alley behind the row of shops, but there was no one in sight. If left ajar, her back door had blown open a time or two when the narrow alley created a wind tunnel. This meant he hadn't even properly closed it before leaving.

"I should call the police station."

The little bundle in her arms screwed up his cherub face and fussed.

"But first, let's see if there's a bottle or pacifier in your diaper bag." Back out front, she picked up the striped bag and put it on the old built-in glass-front display counter, but before she could unzip it, the front door swung wide as Nicholas Weller pushed through with a bag of takeout from the Acorn Café.

He stopped short and his jaw dropped slightly open.

Her well-practiced teacher's stare was achieving the desired reaction. "I can't believe you would do such a thing. How could you be this dumb?" she said quietly enough not to upset the baby.

His eyebrows sprang up toward his perfectly styled light-brown hair, and his broad cocky smile was nowhere to be found.

"I was about to call the police and report you," she said.

Without taking his eyes from her, he slowly set his bag of food on a makeshift table of plywood and two sawhorses. "Catch me up here. Report me for what, exactly?"

"Are you kidding me?" she said so loudly the baby started crying again. "Oh, now look what you've made me do."

This is not at all how today was supposed to go.

Nicholas Weller knew what it was like to have a woman mad at him, but he usually knew the reason. Not this time. Why was his ill-tempered neighbor in his store yelling at him with her crying baby in her arms?

"I'm sorry, sweetie. I didn't mean to startle you," she cooed to the child, then met his eyes again.

Her pink lips pursed above a slightly pointed chin, and what felt like crystal daggers shot from her pale green eyes. Nicholas pressed his lips tight against the untimely urge to laugh. With her hair pulled into a tight bun, she looked like an angry pixie. Weren't people in small towns supposed to be welcoming? And the reason for her uninvited visit was still a mystery. In her primary-colored crayon dress—which was better suited to a child—this prickly, judgmental schoolteacher was going to be a tough neighbor.

"I should report you for leaving your baby alone while you ran out for food."

"Whoa. Wait a minute." Suddenly ice cold to the core, he held up both hands and backed away. "This is not my baby."

"He's not?" She looked between the two of them as if searching for similarities. "Then where did he come from?"

"I thought it was yours."

She made a growling sound in her throat. "He's a baby, not an *it*."

"Where did *he* come from? I was only gone ten minutes."

"I didn't see anyone come in or out of your front door." She gasped. "But I did hear your back door bang and found it wide open."

"It was? I didn't leave it open." Every hair on his body stood at attention. This was getting weirder by the second. "Is someone playing a joke on me? Are there cameras?" He went to the front windows and scanned the area.

"If it's a joke, I'm not in on it." Joining him at the window, she swayed, rocking the tiny infant. "This baby is only a few months old. You've truly never seen this child and have no idea who he belongs to?"

He had to clear his throat twice before he could answer. "No."

The infant made mewling sounds, and she held

him toward Nicholas. "Hold the baby while I see if there's a bottle in the diaper bag."

His pulse jumped, and Nicholas shoved his hands into the front pockets of his gray slacks. "I've never held a baby."

She turned her body away as if that answer deemed him unfit. Cradling the baby in the crook of one arm, she unzipped the bag and pulled out a pacifier. "You need to look in this diaper bag. There's a letter with your name on it."

Had he fallen into a delusion? He'd ask her to pinch him, but she looked to be in more of a slapping mood. After a brief hesitation, he approached the open bag as if it was venomous. On top of diapers and clothes, there was an envelope, and it really did have his name on it.

This can't be good.

"Who is the mother?" Emma asked.

He picked up the ordinary white envelope with the potential to change his life, and it seemed to weigh a hundred pounds. "I have no idea."

She gaped at him and once again clutched the infant closer. "How can you not know who his mother is? Are there that many options?"

"You're assuming he's mine." His throat was so tight it was almost a whisper.

Surely a DNA test will prove this isn't my child.

With a shaky hand, he slid his thumb under the flap, hissing at the sting of a paper cut. Was this minor wound an omen of things to come? He unfolded a page of postpartum instructions from a hospital in Houston, but with no patient name. On the back was a handwritten note of looping script that looked familiar. With his heart slamming against his breastbone, he silently read.

I tried to hide the truth, but the truth found me.
I took the coward's way, I took the pay, and
now you'll see.
Will you ever forgive me?
Looking into his eyes, your eyes, I saw the only
choice can be...
Introducing you to your baby.
And even though it's probably too late to be
a family of three, our baby deserves to know
his family tree.

"Aurora." Blood rushed in his ears as his vision blurred. This poem-style message could only be one person. His ex-girlfriend, Aurora Di Ciano. Poems like this had been her fun way of leaving him messages or clues to solve. And this message was clear.

She had my baby?

She had never said anything about being pregnant. A quick calculation of the last time he'd seen Aurora and the approximate age of the baby would make it possible. It all lined up with the time Aurora abruptly broke up with him. One day he thought he might be falling in love, and the next, she disappeared from his life. Nicholas fumbled in the bag for more information. Proof he wasn't jumping to wild conclusions and this really was Aurora's baby. Moving bottles, diapers and a can of formula, he found a large manila envelope tucked into an inside pocket. He pulled out a cardstock page just far enough to see the baby's footprints. A few more inches revealed a handwritten name.

Nicholas Jackson Weller, Jr. Six pounds twelve ounces & nineteen inches long.

An unfamiliar emotion hit with the force of an ocean wave, bringing with it the sting of salt in his eyes. She'd given the child his name. He held his breath and slid the page out farther, and his suspicion was confirmed.

Mother, Aurora Ann Di Ciano. Father, Nicholas Jackson Weller.

Aurora was not the kind of person who would try to trick him into taking a baby who wasn't his. She was as straightforward as they came and honest— almost to a fault. But where in the hell was she?

"Mr. Weller? Nicholas?"

Snapping his head up, he met Emma's inquisitive eyes. "I'm sorry. What?"

"Are you okay?" she asked and came close enough to put a hand on his shoulder. "You're looking a little pale."

"I'm fine." He was definitely not, but you never let a stranger see weakness or too much emotion.

The page slipped back into its envelope with a barely audible *whoosh*. But one loud enough to change everything. The world as he knew it was over. Something that was never supposed to happen had dropped into his life without any warning. Lord knew he had no example of how to be a parent.

After squeezing his eyes closed and counting to five, he took his first good look at the tiny baby in her arms. Big curious eyes. A little mouth working furiously on a translucent blue pacifier. He reached out for one little foot poking from the folds of a blue blanket, his skin softer than anything he'd ever touched. This time the wave of emotion was gentle but all-consuming, like the heat of a summer day.

"He's mine." He met Emma's gaze. "And before you ask me again, yes, I know who the mother is. The question is, where is she?" He turned in a circle like she'd appear from the scarred and faded woodwork.

"I take it she never told you she was pregnant?"

"No. She just suddenly disappeared from my life." *Why am I telling a stranger these personal details?*

"Could she be the one I heard at the back door?" Emma asked.

"That's not at all like Aurora. I need to call her." He pulled out his phone and walked toward the back office.

While the phone rang, he recalled a message

Aurora left a few months ago saying that she would call back soon. Still licking his wounds from being dumped, he had not tried to call her, hoping to discover how badly she wanted to reconnect. Much to his disappointment, she had not tried to reach him again.

This is what she wanted to tell me, and I was too prideful to call her. Maybe my father is right. I'm too self-absorbed.

"Hello, Nick," said a male voice on the other end of the phone line. "It's me. Marco."

"Marco? Why are you answering your sister's phone? Where is she?" Nicholas heard sniffling and the shuddering breath of restrained crying. "What's wrong?"

"She's gone."

"Where?" His whole body went numb.

"She died."

I couldn't have heard that right. His pulse raced and Nicholas's brain scrambled to turn the teenager's words into something else. Something not horrible.

"She had the baby and then she died. She's gone." The young man's voice was a forced whisper, hoarse with sorrow.

Nicholas propped his forehead against the white shiplap wall, struggling to get air into his lungs. "Marco, where are you?"

"Nearby."

"You brought the baby?"

"Yes."

"Get your butt back over here."

"On my way."

With a deep inhale that didn't help the least little bit, Nicholas stepped out of the empty office. Emma's voice drifted down the hallway, singing a lullaby that tapped at a memory just out of reach. He paused and cocked his head. Someone had sung that song to him. But who? Because it certainly hadn't been his parents.

Emma rocked side to side in a hypnotic rhythm as she sang to the tiny infant cradled in one arm. A tear rolled down her cheek followed by another.

Why is she crying?

He followed the movement of her delicate hand brushing her tears away. She had short, neat, unpainted nails, very unlike the women he was used to dating.

When she saw him, she swiped at her cheek again. "Do we need to call the police?"

"No. I know who brought him." He leaned against the wall, the backs of his eyes prickling with tears that he would not allow to come out in front of a stranger, or anyone for that matter.

The pacifier popped out of the baby's mouth, and he turned his head to nuzzle against Emma's breast.

"This little guy needs to eat," she said.

He concentrated on breathing so he wouldn't pass out. "His name is Nicholas."

Emma gave a short, clipped laugh. "You've already named him after yourself?"

"No." He frowned at her.

This woman is getting under my skin. And not in the fun way.

"His mother named him." He gazed at the curious face of his tiny son and rubbed the heel of one palm across his chest.

Why didn't she tell me she was pregnant? Am I such a horrible prospect for a father that she tried to hide him from me?

The jagged scar on his knuckle reminded him of the time Aurora talked him into hiking. The day he'd first thought he might be feeling something close to love and considering a long-term relationship. Catching his reflection in the glass of the display case, it took him a second to recognize his own face, etched with grief. Nicholas hardened his features into an expressionless mask before facing Emma.

She tilted her head, observing him in a way that told him Emma Blake was the kind of woman who saw too much.

"Let's go next door to my shop. There's a kitchenette in the back. We can make a bottle for him, and you can sit down."

"She's dead." Even to his own ears, his voice sounded robotic and emotionless.

Emma sucked in a sharp breath and her face shifted into an anguished expression that made him suspect she had experience with something he didn't yet understand.

"His mother? She died?"

"Yes."

"I'm so sorry."

Before he could say more, Marco came through the door. His black hair fell over his forehead but couldn't hide red-rimmed eyes, deep brown and expressive just like Aurora's. Nicholas pulled him into a tight hug, then held on to his shoulders and studied his face. "Are you okay?"

"I will be. I'm sorry I didn't call you, and I'm sorry I left baby Nick here like that." The teenager glanced briefly at Emma while tugging at the collar of his T-shirt. "I went into the back to see if there was a place to make a bottle. When I heard someone come in... I don't know what came over me. I panicked. I figured your girlfriend might not want you to have another woman's child."

"I'm not his girlfriend," she said as fast as a hockey puck sliding across ice.

"I hardly know her," Nicholas said, irritated by her rapid denial of a relationship with him. "She owns the business next door."

"Oh." Marco's brow furrowed as he looked between them. "I didn't go far. I went out the back, then around to the front and watched from behind a tree across the street."

"Should I leave?" Emma asked. "Y'all probably have a lot to talk about."

As if in protest to her suggestion, the baby cried full on, his little pink tongue quivering in his wide-open mouth.

Nicholas winced at the high-pitched crying. "Can we make that bottle at your place?"

"Sure, grab the diaper bag and car seat and follow me."

Nicholas and Marco followed her into the dress shop, where a dark-haired woman was helping a customer, but her eyes followed them as they walked through women's clothing to a little back room set up as a kitchen.

"Hold your son while I make the bottle," Emma said.

Nicholas stared at her without moving a muscle, and she rolled her eyes.

"I'll take him," Marco said. "He is my nephew. I'm Marco." He rested the baby on his shoulder, patting his tiny back.

"Nice to meet you. I'm Emma." Everyone except for the baby was silent while she prepared the bottle, then handed it to Marco. "There are cold drinks in the refrigerator. Help yourself." She rotated her beaded bracelet while glancing once more between them and then left them alone.

The men sat at the two-person bistro table at one end of the narrow space. Once the baby was quietly drinking, Nicholas finally found his voice. "Tell me what happened, starting with, why didn't I know she was pregnant?"

"Because of the money."

A sharp, cold sensation slid down his spine. "What money?"

Marco winced. "The money your dad gave her to disappear from your life. He said our parents' prison records couldn't be associated with his or your name."

Nicholas's vision tinted red, his knee bouncing so fast the metal table rattled. He wanted to argue that his father couldn't have done that. But if he could kick his own son out of the family business until he could "prove his worth," of course he'd do this to a woman he barely knew. Anything to protect the family name. "That's why she broke up with me? He paid her off?"

"Yeah. At first, she told your father no, but then he doubled the amount. But the money wasn't the only reason. She knew she'd never be accepted into the Weller family. And she said you'd told her you weren't the kind of guy who ever wanted to settle down and be a family man."

A tight knot formed in his chest. He *had* said that. More than once, partly to remind himself he didn't know how a healthy family really worked. "How did she die?"

"A surgical complication the day after having the baby by C-section."

Nicholas held his breath to fight off a sob he refused to let out. If he had been by her side, would he have seen something was wrong and possibly been able to save her? Could he have prevented her death if he'd been there?

"I didn't put you on the birth certificate because I still thought she didn't want you to know, but then I found the poem she'd written. When they started talking about putting the baby in foster care, I showed them my sister's will listing me as guardian if something should happen to her." He shook his head and adjusted the bottle. "Nothing was supposed to happen. It shouldn't be like this."

"No, it shouldn't." He gritted his teeth against a wave of nausea. "Marco? Why didn't you just call me?"

"I was afraid your father would ask for the money back if he found out that I contacted you. And a lot of it was spent and I needed the rest to take care of the baby." He smiled down at his nephew. "I've tried, but I don't have any idea what I'm doing. My friends have been telling me to put him up for adoption."

"Adoption?" His stomach clenched and rolled. *Oh my God. What am I about to do?* "If he's really mine... I'll take him."

"You can get a DNA test if you want, but I promise he's yours. My sister wasn't seeing anyone but you. She wasn't like that."

"I know. I believe you." Aurora was the only woman who'd ever made him consider a real relationship. Until she'd left him like yesterday's garbage.

"I do have one piece of good news. I got a full-ride football scholarship to UT in Austin," Marco said.

"That's great, kid. Congratulations. Did your sister know?"

"Yes. She was proud." He looked at Nicholas with imploring eyes. "I have some buddies in Austin who said I can live with them, but not with a baby. It's more of a college party house, not exactly a good fit for a newborn. And I really want to take the scholarship and get a degree."

"Of course. Aurora would definitely want you to go to college."

"Do I have to give back what's left of the money?"

"Absolutely not. You keep it. Use it for college expenses."

Marco's shoulders relaxed. "Do you have a lawyer who can help with getting your name on the birth certificate and all that legal stuff? Seems like rich people always do."

He didn't bother saying that it was his parents who were rich. Not so much him anymore without his salary from the auction house—and his habit of overspending instead of saving. He was far from destitute, but he couldn't go throwing money around like he used to. "I know a few lawyers. I'll call one of them."

"His shot record and the pediatrician's information are in the pocket of the diaper bag. The doctor said he is healthy and growing like he should."

"That's good. Sounds like you've done a great job taking care of him. How old is he?" Nicholas couldn't believe he was having to ask the age of his own baby. But the date is not the part he had been focused on when he glanced at the paperwork in the manila envelope. More than that...he couldn't believe he even had a baby.

"Four months. He was born on February first." Marco pulled the bottle from the sleeping baby's mouth, leaving a dribble of milk on his dimpled chin.

Nicholas's hand went reflexively to his own chin and the slight cleft he'd inherited from his grandfather.

"You have to make sure to burp him after he eats." Marco demonstrated how to place the baby on his shoulder and pat his back until they heard a soft burp.

"How do you know how to do this?" Nicholas asked. "Take care of a baby, I mean."

"The internet, and I asked a friend's mom."

If a nineteen-year-old can learn how to do this, I can, too. Right?

He could call his old childhood nanny, but Angela wouldn't be able to do more than give him advice over the phone from her retirement home. Confidence was rarely a problem, but in this case, Nicholas was going to have to ask for help from someone closer by, and only one person came to mind.

Would Emma Blake take pity on him? Or would she laugh in his face?

Chapter Two

Emma didn't mean to hear any of Nicholas and Marco's conversation, but there was no door on the kitchenette, and they weren't exactly whispering. As a kindergarten teacher, she was trained to hear everything going on in her classroom, and while this might not be her school, it was her store.

Was a touch of guilt setting in? Yes, but there was an innocent baby caught up in this tragic mess. But the baby wasn't the only reason she'd chosen to work near the back of the shop while Jenny tended to customers up front. Her brain was in no condition to smile and help someone find a size or put together an outfit. Emma hung another garment on the steamer hook and watched wrinkles release from the white cotton blouse.

"Does he sleep all night?" Nicholas asked.

The younger man chuckled in a sad sort of way. "No. You like coffee?"

"Yes."

"Good. You're going to need it."

The new father's heavy sigh turned into something between a pained groan and determined grunt.

Emma chuckled but quickly sobered, her moment of amusement turning to worry. Nicholas had no idea what he was getting himself into, and his attempt at childcare was bound to be more frightening than comical. This wasn't a puppy they were talking about.

He's going to need help. A lot of help.

Someone without background information would think the men's conversation was the plot of a novel or soap opera. Payoffs, breakups, secret babies, a newborn without a mother, and a father and uncle without a clue of what they were doing. A child's future up in the air.

Nicholas had rejected the mention of putting his son up for adoption, but if his tone of voice was an indication, he hadn't truly convinced himself. She'd never considered adopting a child, but... She was a mother with empty arms, and here was a baby with no mother to hold him.

Maybe it will be too much for him and I can...

Freshly pressed cotton crumpled into a wad in Emma's fist, and fiery talons seized her chest. This razor-sharp pain had been a constant companion for the whole first year. Now, more than three years in, the grief grabbed her less and less but there were times like this that the monster jumped out of hiding with no warning. The fleeting thought of adopting this baby had tapped directly into her fear of loss. She couldn't allow herself even one second of considering this baby could possibly be hers. The danger of such hopes was too high. Too risky.

Why was the world so unfair? So cruel? These men had a baby they didn't ask for and didn't know how to take care of, while she would give anything to hold her baby girl. Anything to sleep beside her husband and raise their daughter together.

Someone touched her shoulder and Emma jumped.

"Feeling guilty about eavesdropping?" Jenny whispered with a grin.

"Maybe a little." With a slow inhale, Emma brushed her fingers across each of the natural-stone beads on her bracelet, just like her therapist suggested. Amethyst and rose quartz for healing. Onyx for letting go of old sorrows. And the small silver rabbit that reminded her of Steven and his nickname for her. Touching each one reminded her to count the blessings she did have.

This was not the time to spiral downward into

thoughts about things she couldn't change. She'd come too far in her healing.

"Come up front so we can talk." Jenny turned off the steamer and hooked an arm through hers. "Are you getting in your head?"

"Nope. Not going there."

"Good."

They walked all the way to the front window display she'd been staging before being sidetracked by the baby's crying.

"What in the world is going on with them?" Jenny hitched a thumb toward the back.

"A surprise baby," Emma whispered.

"No way. You're messing with me."

"I swear I'm not. Apparently, Nicholas Weller had a girlfriend who got pregnant but never told him. And then she died."

Jenny clasped both hands to her chest. "Oh, no. That's horrible."

"And Nicholas has *no* idea what he's doing as far as a baby goes. He's never even held one."

"Wow. What were they saying? What happens now?"

"Now who's interested in the eavesdropping?" Emma grinned and put a wide-brimmed floppy hat on the mannequin with the new red-and-white dress.

"It's hard to resist a good story," Jenny said.

"The younger one, who is the uncle, is going to go

to college in Austin. He's leaving the baby in Nicholas's very incapable hands."

"And you're not about to let that baby be put in any danger."

"True. But what in the world can I do?"

Jenny tapped one lavender-polished fingertip against her lips. "Hmm. Well…"

Before they could come up with an idea, the men came up to the front of the shop. Mixed in with obvious sadness, there was a faraway, glazed look on Nicholas's face.

Marco kissed the baby's forehead. "I love you. I might not know how to be a father, but I'll be the best uncle I can." He prepared to hand the baby to Nicholas, who shot a panicked look toward Emma.

Are you kidding me? Emma inhaled a calming breath and took the sleeping baby from the young uncle.

"Thanks for helping him," Marco said to Emma.

She opened her mouth to say she wasn't doing anything for Nicholas Weller, but the slight weight of the precious baby in her arms took over her mouth without her brain's permission. "Sure. No problem."

No problem? What am I saying?

Marco gripped the older man's shoulders. "I'll call you later and give you my new address in Austin. I'm only an hour and a half away, and I can come see y'all often."

"That's good."

"I'm going to move my car closer and give you a few more of baby Nick's things," Marco said. With one more tenderhearted glance at his nephew, the young man walked out the door.

Silence and anxiety hung heavy in the air. With tension hardening his jaw and neck, you could almost feel the vibrations of distress rolling off the new dad.

Emma adjusted the baby in her arms. "Nicholas, this is my business partner, Jenny McKnight."

"It's nice to meet you," he said in a detached, wooden voice. "I'm going to step outside and get the rest of the baby's stuff." He walked out onto the sidewalk and looked both ways without choosing either.

Emma and Jenny looked at one another, having a whole silent conversation within seconds—in the way only good friends can.

There was no getting out of spending time with Nicholas. He needed help. A lot of help. "I can't just send this baby off with him." Emma turned for the back. "I'm going to change his diaper."

Moving aside her laptop and file folders, Emma spread a changing pad on her desk. "Let's get a fresh diaper on you, little sweetie." She laughed when he stuck out his tongue and couldn't resist leaning down to kiss his forehead. "I promise you'll feel better with a clean bottom." He pushed his little feet against her hand and grunted, all while staring at her with dark, curious eyes. He was strong and alert with a fine fuzz of dark hair and was just about the cutest thing ever.

Once he was freshly clean and swaddled in his blanket, she cradled him against her chest and inhaled the intoxicating baby scent that no one could bottle. "Let's go see if your daddy is back." She got to the front of the shop just as Nicholas came through the doorway holding a white bassinet with a large shopping bag sitting in it.

"Can I talk to you about something, please?" he asked Emma.

"Sure." This time she took him into the office across from the kitchenette and closed the door.

Nicholas set the baby items on the floor in front of her desk. "I… Would you…" He rubbed the back of his neck while looking at the beadboard ceiling. "Oh, hell. I need help."

It had obviously taken a lot for him to ask her for help, and she didn't disagree with his statement. "Tell me what kind of help you need."

"I don't even know. That's a big part of the problem."

Oh, boy, this is going to be even more work than I anticipated.

Nicholas was having trouble breathing and wasn't sure how he'd even found the air in his lungs to form words and ask for help. He'd just blurted it out without thinking through the request. But he needed someone who knew what they were doing, and he needed them right now. There was no time to interview and hire a nanny.

What was he even asking her to do? He didn't know Emma Blake. Not really. And if she hadn't found the baby, it never in a million years would've crossed his mind to seek out the prickly woman he'd met at the small-business owners' meeting. The one who all but growled at him every time they were within eyesight. Interacting with other people she was the picture of friendly, but with him... He'd done something or reminded her of someone who'd hacked her off in a big way.

Emma stroked the curve of the infant's head. "Do you live alone?"

"Yes. Alone." Nicholas caught Emma's eye and prayed he didn't look pathetic, because he felt adrift and headed for his own secluded island. "I don't know anything about taking care of a baby."

"So I gathered." She hit him with a judgmental expression, but when he rubbed a hand over the tight band of tension around his chest, her features softened into the semblance of a smile. "I suppose I can give you a few pointers."

"I'd appreciate that." He braced himself against the wall and concentrated on breathing. Passing out was not an option. When his parents got word of this, they were going to flip out—in the most passive-aggressive and proper sort of way. This kind of "situation" did not fit the image they were so desperate to project. Maybe their sending him off to prove his worth was a blessing in disguise. There was way less chance of anyone finding out about the baby while he was in this small Texas Hill Country town. He needed time to figure out how to handle this mammoth surprise.

Alone in the tiny office with Emma, Nicholas ran a hand roughly across his head, not caring that he'd messed up his hair. "I don't know what happens next."

She settled into the chair behind the desk—which he recognized as a valuable Edwardian piece—and eyed him suspiciously. "Are you thinking about giving him up for adoption?"

"No!" Her words made his stomach roil. Adoption was great for some people, but he couldn't hand his baby over to strangers. His parents had not given him away, but they'd handed him over to the nanny who raised him. "That does not mean I know how to take care of him. I didn't even know how to make the bottle."

She started to say something but pressed her lips together and looked at the sleeping baby in her arms.

"Do you know a lot about taking care of a baby?" he asked.

Her throat bobbed a few times. "Yes."

The effort used to say that one word hinted at a life familiar with pain, and his emotions once again punched him in the gut. What had she experienced?

"Don't you have family who can help you out with the baby?"

"No." He didn't elaborate. This woman didn't need to hear his sob story. He hated it when people felt sorry for him.

"Friends?"

"Not locally." His single buddy at the vineyard had helped him find and buy his retail space but wouldn't be any help in this case. "Would you consider a deal where we help one another out?"

"What kind of deal?" she asked with narrowed eyes.

"I could pay you to be his nanny."

She motioned to the laptop and stack of papers on one end of the desk. "I do have a business to run."

"I understand. What about something short-term until I can find a nanny?" She was already so protective over the baby, if he could just get her to start, maybe she'd want to continue helping him for longer. "What about one week?"

"Do you want me to take care of your son or teach *you* to take care of him?"

"Both?" He attempted one of his signature smiles—which usually made women giggle or swoon—but this time... It failed to obtain the desired result. Her expression was more of an I'm-not-impressed look, but he couldn't give up now. He had no other prospects because he was most definitely not running back to Houston with a mess to clean up. He would not return until he'd proved himself. Not until his new business was open and he could find a competent manager to run the gallery and wine bar. Only then could he return to his position at Weller's Auction House and prepare to someday take over the reins.

Nicholas cleared his throat and tried again. "One week of baby lessons for however much you want. A crash course. Name a price."

Her pretty cat eyes tipped up at the corners and narrowed on him. "What if I don't want money?"

"Then you'd be a rare kind of person."

"What do you have to bargain with, Mr. Nicholas Weller?"

He thought for a moment, but nothing came to mind. "I don't know." Her sigh was long and drawn out, much like the extended version of the Italian opera his mother insisted he sit through.

"Okay. One week of lessons. You're just lucky that today was the last day and school is out for the summer," she said. "We can work out the details of our deal. I have a garage that needs painting."

"I can paint."

The tilt of her head suggested she didn't believe him. "Where do you live?"

"I haven't found a house, yet. I'm still at the extended-stay hotel near the highway."

"That won't be a very convenient place to give lessons or to live with a newborn. You'll need a full kitchen." She absently stroked the baby's head. "For now, why don't we go to my house, and I can start teaching you some of the basics."

"I'd really appreciate that."

"Well, no time like the present. Let's get going." Emma crossed to the kitchenette and gently placed the sleeping child in the carrier. After rearranging the blanket to buckle the straps between the baby's little legs and over his shoulders, she pulled the carrying handle into place with a click.

He glanced over his shoulder at the bassinet full of baby gear sitting in front of the desk. "I guess I should put all the baby's things in my car."

"In your two-seater convertible?"

"Yes. It has a trunk."

"We can't all fit in it. The car seat has to be buckled in, and a back seat is best. You do know you'll have to get a different car, right?"

His jaw dropped, then clenched. "Get rid of my classic Corvette? I just finished restoring it. And I did all the work myself."

"Well, I don't know what to tell you about that." She looked him up and down as if judging his wardrobe choices. "You worked on a car yourself?"

"Yes. I did. Where's your car?" he asked.

"I walked. I only live a few blocks away. We'll take the diaper bag now and come back for the rest later." She lifted the car seat and walked to the front of the shop. "Jenny, will you be okay by yourself for the rest of the afternoon?"

"Yes, of course. Call me later," said the woman with long dark hair.

At least a walk would burn off some of the sudden stress and nervous energy churning inside him. Nicholas slung the diaper bag over his shoulder and followed Emma outside. "I should check the back door in my shop and make sure everything is locked up before we go." He held the door for her to go through first. His late lunch from the café still sat there, cold and unappetizing, and his stomach was in no shape to accept the cheeseburger with jalapeños and bacon.

Still unnerved by today's surprise, he checked every space, including closets, to make sure no one was inside. Once his property was secured, they started across the historic town square. More than one person turned to stare at them or whisper to a companion. He'd never minded being the center of attention, but today, it felt too intrusive, like everyone could see his shortcomings.

Emma shifted the infant carrier to her other hand.

"I'll carry Jax," he said. "That baby seat looks heavy."

"Jax?"

Her grin was friendly, and he relaxed just a fraction. Nicholas took the baby from her, gripping the handle as if the carrier contained priceless art. He'd never thought about it, but gazing at this tiny human, he realized there was nothing more priceless than a baby.

"Jax is short for his middle name, Jackson. Like mine. That's what my childhood nanny called me." Angela had been with the Weller family most of his life, and he still enjoyed her company more than most of the people who shared his last name.

Jax cooed and flung uncoordinated little arms above his head for a stretch.

"Hey there, little man." This was his first time holding his son. It wasn't so scary with the baby cradled safely in his car seat, but holding his tiny body without all this support was a much more intimidating prospect.

"Do you have sisters or brothers?" Emma asked.

"One sister. She is five years older. I think the only reason my parents had a second child was because my father wanted an heir to carry on his last name."

"Well, you have accomplished that."

Beyond the town square, a neighborhood stretched toward the west. They passed historic homes lined up like a timeline, dating back over a hundred years. Victorian, Tudor, Craftsman and then mid-century. Mature trees lined the sidewalks, light sifting through the rustling leaves and watery colors bleeding into one another like a Georgia O'Keefe landscape painting.

This was a new world where he didn't know the rules or how to navigate the terrain.

The homes and yards were all well-tended. One was even being painted as they walked by. *McKnight Restoration* was written along the bed of a work truck loaded with ladders and buckets. It was the same company he'd hired to work on his gallery. What art or antiques might be hiding in some of these houses? Things the owners didn't know were valuable. Maybe he could go back to Houston with impressive new pieces.

They walked in silence, with him trying to make sense of the disorienting turn the day had taken and her probably cursing the day he'd come to town. He would not be heading to Austin to meet the woman his friend had set him up with. He would not be staying out late and sleeping in the next morning. Who knew when he'd ever be able to date or go out with friends again?

Halfway down Cedar Lane, Emma opened the gate of an honest-to-God white picket fence. A brick pathway curved around a flower bed and up to a white midcentury ranch house on a wooded lot.

"Nice place," he said. "Do you know if there are any houses for rent in this neighborhood?"

"I know of a small garage apartment."

"Where is it?"

She pointed toward the back of her house. "Above my garage."

Was this his good fortune? Nicholas couldn't decide.

Chapter Three

Emma bit down hard on the inside of her cheek, unlocked her front door and motioned for Nicholas to come inside. Why had she told him her apartment was vacant? If he wanted to rent it, they'd be neighbors both at work and at home. He'd probably expect maid service and home-cooked meals.

With the car seat clutched in one hand, Nicholas followed her across the entryway and through a pocket door to the galley-style kitchen. He set his sleeping son's carrier on the round table at one end of the room. His hand hovered above the baby like he'd touch him, but he didn't, and his expression stayed neutral.

Does he have no feelings for his own child?

Emma studied the well-put-together man before her, and her annoyance softened. On the inside, he was likely freaking out. Who wouldn't be? Becoming a father in a matter of minutes. Needing a stranger's help. And mourning a woman he might have loved.

Fiery talons once again gripped her heart. She of all people understood loss. She would've been completely adrift without her friends and family to help her through the most devastating thing she could imagine. What Nicholas needed was understanding and comfort. He needed a friend.

He looked up from the baby and then around the kitchen from the pale-turquoise backsplash to the reproduction '50s-era appliances. "You've updated it but kept the midcentury style."

Was that a compliment?

"Except that I opened up part of that wall to the living room. I wanted to be able to cook and still…" Her throat tightened, trapping the rest of her words. There might be questions if she admitted doing it in anticipation of working in the kitchen while keeping an eye on her child.

"So you can interact with your guests?" Nicholas asked, his deep voice bringing her out of her thoughts.

"Yes, exactly. I had to sacrifice a few upper cabinets, but it was worth it. Now I can see the TV." She could also see the sunny space under the windows where she'd envisioned a play area with a bookshelf and baskets of toys.

I need to stop thinking about what could have been.

Nicholas rubbed a palm against his perfectly structured jaw, and even she had to admit he was a good-looking guy. The kind who makes it onto the cover of *GQ* or an underwear ad. A tingle started in her belly. One she hadn't felt with anyone since her husband. Why now? Why this man?

The baby made snuffling sounds in his sleep, and she made herself look away from his father.

"Is the apartment furnished?" he asked.

"Partially. There's a couch, dining table, dresser and bookshelf. But no bed. Although the couch folds out."

And it's uncomfortable as hell.

One of her students' favorite fairy tales, *The Princess and the Pea*, came to mind. Would Prince Nicholas complain about the metal bar digging into his back through the flimsy mattress like the princess complained about a tiny pea? Emma couldn't stop her grin. "Want to see the apartment?"

"Please. It would be nice to get out of the hotel."

"Let me grab the key. And you bring Jax." She pulled a key ring from a drawer by the sink and went out the back kitchen door near the table.

Glancing at the row of trees she'd planted to honor her husband and daughter, she pressed her hand to her heart as she always did, sending a silent *I love you* to heaven. More and more this ritual gave her a sense of peace and connection. It felt good to smile and laugh again.

With the rhythm of Nicholas's steps, Jax had drifted off and the pacifier dropped from the sleeping baby's mouth. Emma looked up the length of his father's arm. He carried the car seat as if it weighed nothing. Even in a dress shirt, muscles stood out and strained the fabric along his bicep. He wasn't the bulky, muscle-bound type, but he was tall and leanly muscled. She'd bet money there was a nice body hiding under the Prada and Gucci.

"This is the garage you want painted?" he asked.

"Yes. Think you can handle that?"

"I know I can. If you'll watch the baby while I do it?" he said with a lopsided, mischievous grin.

She laughed, despite her aggravation. "I suppose I'll have to."

Nicholas came up the stairs behind her, and she could almost feel his gaze on her as she unlocked the apartment door. "I know it's hot in here right now, but the air conditioner works well."

He walked to the center of the open-concept living, dining and kitchen space and turned in a circle, taking in everything in a way that suggested she'd be getting an inspection report.

Surely, a guy like him wouldn't want to stay in this tiny one-bedroom for long. "This probably isn't at all what you're used to, but it's clean and available. I recently painted the walls and installed a new backsplash and countertop."

"It will work. I'll take it."

Again, not much of a compliment, but what did she expect? She'd seen enough of his clothes, shoes and watches to know he was used to fine things.

After a quick peek at the bedroom that was barely large enough for a full-size bed and the compact bathroom, they went back to her house and the comfort of the air-conditioning.

Her stomach growled loud enough to be heard across the room. "I'm hungry, and I know you didn't get to eat your lunch. I have leftover pasta with pesto sauce if you want some?"

"Yes, please. I'm suddenly starving." He sat at the table with the car seat at his feet. "He'll be okay sleeping in this?"

"Yes, as long as we can see him, but it's definitely not a good long-term solution. Luckily you already have the bassinet." She got out the glass container of leftovers and put it into the microwave. "We can eat while the baby is asleep. Getting things done while he's sleeping is something you'll need to do. Although, at this age when they're not sleeping through the night, it's probably better to rest when he does." She outright grinned at the slightly horrified expression on his face.

"I guess it's hard to get much done with a baby.

Probably why my parents employed a full-time nanny."

Which is obviously what he planned to do. He'd already asked her to take the job. "It can be a lot. I've taken care of two foster babies."

That had been before she was pregnant. But since… She couldn't bring herself to take in another baby. It was too painful. This current situation had been thrust upon her, however, and baby Jax needed her too much for her to say no this time.

She divided the heated leftovers into two bowls. "Grab a drink from the refrigerator." Would he pick juice, a soft drink, beer or water?

His hand hovered over a bottle of beer before grabbing a cola. "What can I get for you?"

"I'll take the same as you. We're probably going to need the jolt of caffeine."

Sitting across from Nicholas was easier than she'd thought it would be. Thank goodness he was turning out to be a mostly normal guy, if a touch high maintenance. There had been no demands to be served, but still, she got the feeling that was exactly what he was used to.

"This is really good," he said.

"Thanks." *Wow, an actual compliment.*

He worked his fork and spoon expertly to twirl another bite of pasta. He'd been working with those hands. Two scraped knuckles, calluses on his palms and a swatch of blue that might be paint or ink. His nails weren't raggedy, but they weren't perfectly manicured, either. Nicholas wasn't the man she'd first thought he was. It could be the shock of sudden fatherhood had sucked the haughtiness right out of him. Could be he wasn't putting on the public face she'd seen him use on several occasions.

"I think you've met Tess Curry, who runs the antique store across the square from our shops?" she asked.

"Yes. She has some nice pieces and a good eye."

"She told me you work at your family's auction house and know a lot about art."

His fork dropped into his bowl, and he waited a beat before he met her gaze. "I did work there. Weller's was started by my great-grandfather, and I have a degree in art history."

His eyes were a little sad and a deep rich green, darker than her moss-colored eyes. And if she wasn't mistaken, mentioning the auction house had darkened his mood. What had happened to make him leave the family business? "So, what brought you to Oak Hollow?"

"A friend owns one of the wineries in the Hill Country. Deco Vineyard. Philip Deco wants a tasting room in town, and I was looking for a new... business opportunity."

"I've been to Deco Vineyard. It's really nice."

"One of the best in the area. We're combining art and wine."

With her head tipped, she smiled at him. "That's actually a good idea."

He chuckled. "You sound so surprised."

Maybe his gallery would be better than she'd first thought. A tasting room would certainly bring in customers, but that meant she had even less of a chance of ever getting his retail space for their expansion.

His cell phone rang, and he looked at the screen with an uneasy expression. "It's my father. I need to take this." He answered the call on his way out the back door.

She stood at the sink and washed their bowls while Nicholas paced across her backyard, his body language screaming with tension. There was definitely something going on between him and his family.

Jax whimpered, then started crying.

"Hey there, sweetie pie." She kneeled beside him to rub his tummy, and he grabbed her fingers with surprising strength. "Are you ready to have some fun with your daddy? I think he needs a distraction from some of the heavy and sad stuff he's dealing with, and we should start with a lesson in diaper changing."

The baby arched his back and grunted.

She laughed. "Are you playing along and making a dirty diaper? What a good boy."

Emma put the changing pad on the carpet in front of her fireplace, then set out baby wipes and a fresh diaper. Nicholas came in just as she lifted Jax from his carrier and centered him on the pad. She stepped back and waved her arm like a showroom model. "Time to change your first diaper."

"Don't you want to demonstrate first?"

His puppy-dog eyes were not going to work on her. Not even when they were framed with thick, dark lashes. "I'll talk you through it. Start by un-snapping his onesie."

Kneeling at his son's feet, Nicholas rested his hands on his thighs and looked things over. "I'm guessing a onesie is the thing he's wearing?"

"Yes." *Oh, boy. Super novice.* He was going to be a needy student.

Between the baby's chubby little legs, he pulled the snaps apart, then folded the cloth up and out of the way. "Now what?"

"Pull back those tabs on each side of the diaper. They're like Velcro. Then open the diaper and see what horror awaits you."

He jerked his head to gape at her and caught her laughing. "Very funny," he said. "But you are kidding, right?"

"One never knows." She wiggled her eyebrows and couldn't stop her grin.

With a deep breath, he turned back to his challenge.

This week was not going to be the relaxing, self-pampering time she had planned, but there was the potential for this experience to be somewhat entertaining. Emma already had a few ideas for initiating this new father. But it was all in good fun and to occupy his mind with something other than the loss of his baby's mother.

Nicholas stared down at the tiny baby. His baby. Some new section of his heart sprang open. With chocolate-drop eyes too big for his face and a perfect little mouth sucking on two middle fingers, Jax was a cute little guy. But so vulnerable. So fragile.

"You can do it," Emma said and sat on the chaise lounge part of the sectional sofa. "Just take it one step at a time."

Nicholas flashed to the time his mother had taught him to handle fine crystal. Slow movements. A gentle hand. Lightly grasping the baby's soft little feet, he attempted to straighten his legs, but the second he let go, they instantly sprang back like a little frog.

If I can rebuild a classic car, I can do this.

Careful not to use too much strength, he worked around his chubby little legs, peeled back the tabs, opened the diaper and breathed a sigh of relief that it was only wet. It contained no horrors or smells to make him gag.

But as he leaned over him, the tiny baby shot a stream of pee alarmingly high and directly onto the front of his shirt. Reaction time slowed by surprise, he folded the diaper back into place too late to save his newest Calvin Klein shirt. Still a bit stunned, it took him a moment to register the sound of laughter.

Emma had a hand to her stomach and the other over her mouth. She kneeled beside Nicholas, waved him away and took over. "Just watch," she said between giggles.

While unbuttoning his wet shirt, he observed the steps: Wipe all the baby's parts. Slide a fresh diaper under his little bottom and secure it. Not too tight, but not too loose.

Emma was still chuckling as she snapped the onesie. "Sorry I laughed at you, but you should've seen the look on your face. Priceless new-dad moment. Too bad I didn't have a camera rolling."

"Priceless? More like an initiation by peeing squad."

While the baby played with his feet and happily cooed, Emma grabbed the wadded-up wet diaper and walked around into the kitchen to wash her hands. "You'll get the hang of it."

Nicholas was pulling off his shirt when she turned to look at him.

"It's—" Her eyes widened, and she paused mid-sentence.

Smart enough to know better, he didn't smile or say a word about her appraising glance. He wasn't a complete fool, and her reaction was very gratifying. He worked hard to stay in good shape, and he had no problem with her appreciation.

"You're going to have to wear a shirt to go into Target," she said with her eyes cast toward the floor. "Put your shirt in my laundry room for now."

He followed her pointed finger to the small room behind an accordion-style door and draped the shirt over the deep sink beside the stacked washer and dryer. "I'll take care of my shirt tomorrow."

"You need more diapers, formula and other feeding supplies, a stroller and a bunch of other stuff."

"Whoa." He held up a hand. "One thing at a time. First, I need to go to my hotel room to get a clean shirt."

"I'll give you a T-shirt to wear."

He allowed his gaze to travel from her graceful neck to the curve of her waist and hoped he hadn't lingered too long on her breasts. But she *had* checked him out only moments ago. "I don't think your T-shirt will fit me."

"I have one from a school event that's way too big. I'll go get it. Watch the baby."

Jax was still happily entertaining himself with his toes when Nicholas sat on the floor beside him and looked around her living room. A mix of mid-century and newer pieces filled the large airy space. It was becoming obvious that she had a thing for the color blue, especially turquoise. There was a wedding photo on the mantel. Emma was gazing up at a man with black hair and an olive complexion, the opposite to her pale green eyes and blond hair. He looked like he could be a sibling to Aurora and Marcus. There had been no mention or sign of a husband. Not at the small-business owners' meeting or at her shop or around town. There were no men's boots by the back door or a second car in the driveway.

Surely, she wouldn't keep up a photo of an ex-husband.

The baby's legs started working in tandem like a bunny trying to hop.

"You should warn a guy before you pee on him, little man." Jax grabbed Nicholas's finger and tried to pull it to his mouth. "You're pretty strong for your size. Your momma must be—"

He sucked in a sharp breath that caught in his dry throat and the backs of his eyes burned. He'd been so focused on the baby that he hadn't truly allowed himself to think too much about Aurora. Sweet, kind Aurora who had raised her kid brother.

She would've been such a good mother.

"I'll tell you all about your mom, and so will your uncle Marco. She was a wonderful woman with many talents."

Later, when he was alone in the shower, he could allow tears to fall for the woman whom he might have loved and shared a life with. That's the only place he ever allowed that much emotion to come out.

Emma returned to the living room and tossed a bright purple shirt at him.

Holding it out before him, he studied the cartoon

bear under the words *Oak Hollow Elementary.* "I'm not wearing this in public. Isn't Target out by the hotel? We can stop there first, and I can grab a clean shirt."

"Fine, Mr. High Maintenance. We'll stop and get one of your designer shirts. Are you going to go shirtless until then?"

If there was a husband around, surely she would've offered something of his. With a deep sigh, he pulled the garish shirt over his head and wrestled it down his torso. "It's a bit tight."

Lips pressed together to contain another laugh, she cleared her throat. "Maybe the shirt isn't as big as I thought, but it will have to do for now. Let me show you how to make a bottle before we go. We'll probably need it."

Emma parked her dark blue car in front of his hotel. "Do you want to go ahead and pack and check out while we're here?"

Even though he'd originally pegged Emma as judgmental and difficult, she was kind and thoughtful enough to offer to wait in the car with Jax while he packed. "You don't mind waiting?"

"If I let you come back alone, you might never be seen again."

Or maybe not so thoughtful after all. Her expression was one he hadn't yet learned to read, and he wasn't sure whether to be offended or entertained.

"Funny," he said, hoping she was joking. "I promise I'll be back." He got out of Emma's car and rushed to his room before anyone saw him in the ridiculous teddy bear T-shirt.

Inside the store, they got two shopping carts, one for the baby's car seat and one for their purchases.

"Mrs. Blake," a little girl called out and ran their way. Her blond hair was in a high ponytail, and when she got close, Nicholas recognized that she had Down syndrome.

Emma held out her arms for a hug around her waist. "Hello, Hannah. You look so pretty in your pink dress."

"Tank you." Hannah spun around, making her full skirt flare. "You pretty, too."

"Thanks. Who are you here with this evening?"

"Momma." Hannah pointed to her mom paying at the closest register.

Nicholas recognized her mother as Tess Curry, the woman from the antique shop on the town square.

Tess waved from her spot in the checkout line, her other hand pressed against her pregnant belly. She glanced between him and Emma and grinned wide enough to show off big dimples, then made the well-known motion for Emma to call her. And that was no doubt because he was with her, and her friend wanted the latest gossip.

The little girl gasped and peered into the shopping cart. "You got a baby?"

"He's not mine. He's my…" Emma met Nicholas's eyes. "He's my friend's baby. This is Mr. Weller and his son, Jax."

"So cute." The little girl giggled and waved at Jax. "I wuv babies."

Her excitement made him smile.

"My momma has a baby in her tummy." Hannah held out her hand to Nicholas. "Hi, big man."

He chuckled and shook her little hand. "Hello. Glad to meet you, Hannah."

"Bye-bye." With a bright smile, the little girl made her way back to her mother by hopping from one square floor tile to another.

"She's one of my past students," Emma said and veered toward the back of the store. "Hannah always lights up a room, and even though I try not to have a favorite student, she's mine."

"You like teaching?" he asked.

"I do, but I'm thinking about giving it up to build my business with Jenny. She's very talented and made the dress Hannah was wearing. Jenny also designs for a fashion house in Dallas." Emma stopped in a long aisle of disposable diapers. "The vintage shop was my grandmother's, and I loved being there with her. It's where my true passion lies."

"Then you should do it." He couldn't remember anyone ever telling him to follow his passion. The advice he'd received from his family had been more to the tune of do as I do.

While several people said hello and others stared at them with varying degrees of curiosity, they loaded the cart with baby items he didn't even know existed. A Diaper Genie, which he wished could do the dirty deed for him, a fancy baby monitor, a sling contraption to wear the baby on your body and a bottle sanitizer.

"Do you know everyone?" Nicholas asked Emma after she spoke to another customer about their sick mother.

"Not everyone, but Oak Hollow isn't that big, and I've lived here most of my life. Other than the five years I was away for college."

"Who is that?" he asked and pointed to an older gentleman who was pushing a cart full of baking supplies.

"Mr. Bailey. He is dating my business partner's grandmother."

"And that young couple over by the shoes?"

"Hmm. I don't know them. They must be visiting or new in town." She dropped another package of diapers into the cart. "What kind of art are you planning to put in your gallery?"

"Paintings, sculptures and maybe a few other things."

"What about featuring some local artists?"

He had a strong urge to groan. "It's not really going to be the kind of place for crochet or quilts."

"Snobby much?" she asked but chuckled. "That's not what I'm talking about. But there are some women in town who make quilts worthy of being in an art gallery."

He didn't like being thought of as a snob. "You have my interest piqued. What kind of art are you talking about?"

"I know a woman who makes beautiful blown glass, several painters and jewelry makers, and I bet if I show you Nan Curry's needlework, you'll want a piece from her."

"I'd like the opportunity to connect with them and see their work."

"Excellent choice." She smiled and then leaned into the basket to adjust the baby's blanket.

On the way home, they stopped by the gallery and picked up the baby items Marco had brought, and Nicholas drove his Corvette back to Emma's house and parked in the driveway beside her Volvo SUV.

"Let's unload all of your purchases into my house for unpacking and lessons on how to use everything. But first, you should take your belongings up to the apartment and turn on the air-conditioning," Emma said. "I'll take Jax inside with me."

"Thanks. Just leave the baby stuff in your car and I'll unload all of it." He took his suitcases up to his new temporary home and turned on the air conditioner. He'd stayed in hotel rooms bigger than this whole apartment, but it was clean and nicely remodeled. Nicholas rushed back downstairs and unloaded her car. After one more diaper change that was much worse than the first and actually did make him dry heave, he was in need of a stiff drink that he wasn't going to get.

"It's time to hold your son. Sit and get comfortable," Emma said. "You've seen how I hold him."

This time making an extra effort not to show any signs of alarm or unease, Nicholas sat in the teal velvet high-back chair and held his breath as Emma placed the baby in his arms. He caught the scent of baby formula, diaper wipes and sun-warmed flowers from Emma's hair, still pulled back in a knot.

Jax was wrapped in his blue blanket and seemed to weigh almost nothing.

So why does it feel like there's a boulder on my chest?

Emma kept standing there, watching and judging as if she was grading him like one of her students. He remained perfectly still, unwilling to risk a mistake in front of her.

"I'm going to change clothes and then tackle opening some of this baby gear." She motioned to the stack of purchases, then left them alone.

"Well, kid, it looks like you and me need to figure this thing out. I hope you're ready to be a team player." He unfolded the soft blanket to admire more of his son's tiny features.

Jax grabbed his daddy's thumb and tried to get it into his mouth.

Lifting the baby in a slow, smooth motion, Nicholas kissed his forehead. He usually took his time before getting attached to anyone, if he got attached at all, but his protective barriers were melting like cotton candy in the rain. This tiny creature was kind of magical. A whole brand-new person. And it was up to him to make sure he became a successful, responsible adult. The enormous weight of that responsibility made his chest tight.

Logically, he knew he should wait for results of a DNA test and his name to be put on the birth certificate before getting too attached, but feelings didn't wait for permission. And he truly could not imagine Aurora trying to pass off a baby who wasn't his. Was it possible his parents would be different with a grandchild than they had been with him or his sister? Although he knew they would not change a diaper, would they want to spend time with Jax?

Emma returned, and he did an actual double take. Her long hair was loose and falling around her shoulders in blond waves, softening her features and sending out a new vibe. Gone was the boldly printed teacher's dress, and the pair of black yoga pants and fitted pink T-shirt showed off more curves than he'd suspected. In a snap, she'd gone from not-his-type to can-I-have-your-number. The schoolteacher had been put away for the summer, and the woman before him was…tempting as hell.

He marveled once again at how differently his day had turned out from the original plan. This might not be the night out on the town he had envisioned, but he had met a new woman. Emma was not at all who he'd first thought she'd be. She was kind and funny and more attractive than he'd realized. But what intrigued him the most was the way she didn't take any of his excuses or let him get away with things. She called him on it instead.

Don't even think about trying to get her into bed!

She was not his biggest fan and making her mad was not a good place to start. He needed her help, not her companionship. But most importantly, Jax needed Emma.

"What?" she asked with her hands fisted on her curvy hips. "Why are you looking at me like you've never seen me?"

"I've never seen you with your hair down. It's pretty." He blinked and rubbed his eyes. "Can I use your restroom?"

"Sure. Down the hallway."

Nicholas stood and let her take the baby from his arms, surprising himself by instantly missing the slight weight. He made his way down the hall, opened a door and froze. It was not a bathroom. It was a pink room with a baby bed, bunny rabbit mobile and a floral-upholstered rocking chair. After seeing her in tight yoga pants, he was pretty sure she wasn't pregnant, and judging by the fine layer of dust on the bookshelf by the door, this room had not been touched in a while.

Hanging above a changing table was a framed photo of Emma, heavily pregnant, cradling her belly and smiling, sunlight streaming in the window behind her and making the edges of her glow as if she was lit from within. So beautiful, and with a smile he'd yet to see. And this was a likely explanation for why he'd caught her crying as she sang to Jax. Feeling as if he was invading her privacy, he eased the door closed. This could only mean one thing.

Emma had lost her baby.

Chapter Four

Emma swaddled the blanket around baby Jax, relieved to have caught Nicholas smiling and quietly talking to his son, admiring his tiny fingers and toes, his little round tummy and squeezable chubby legs. Maybe he wasn't an emotionless robot after all. But when he'd looked at her, his smile had slipped away, replaced by a moment of what she'd read as confusion before reverting to his *I don't want you to know what I'm thinking* expression.

The baby's eyes fluttered closed, and she nestled him in his bassinet. Emma glanced up when Nicholas returned to the room. "He's asleep," she whispered.

Joining her beside the bassinet, he gazed at his son. "Babies are so tiny. So helpless."

The way he said it, Emma thought maybe he was the one feeling helpless.

"So, throughout the night…" He flexed his fingers, then rubbed his palms against his thighs. "What do I need to do or know? Isn't there something about not letting a baby sleep on his back?"

"The opposite actually."

He mumbled something under his breath and spread his long fingers across his forehead as if willing away a headache.

Out of concern for the baby's safety—more so than the father—she could not send Jax off with him for an overnight. After tomorrow's baby lessons, she'd decide whether or not he could be trusted to safely care for his own infant throughout the night. Yes, she knew it was bold and presumptuous to put herself in charge but putting herself in charge was what made her a good teacher and business owner.

"Since it's getting late and you haven't set up your apartment, Jax can stay here with me tonight. I'll put the bassinet beside my bed."

"Really? You'd do that for me?" His shoulders dropped into a somewhat relaxed position.

"I'll do it for the baby."

His mouth quirked up at one corner. "Got it. For the baby."

And for her own sake, because she'd get no sleep

for worrying about Jax being alone with a child-care novice. Nicholas knew the offer to keep the baby wasn't for his sake and didn't seem offended. That was a plus in his favor, and hopefully meant he wasn't a completely spoiled rich guy who was used to always being pampered and waited on.

Even though she had hoped he would argue and want to take his son upstairs with him, the man wanted a full-time nanny and she'd known he'd take her up on the offer. This tiny baby deserved someone who would love him with every part of themselves. With all the love in the world. Someone who would make a home for him, preferably with more than a foldout couch and empty bedroom.

Standing so close to Nicholas was making her edgy in a way she didn't want to give a name to, so Emma headed into the kitchen. "Do you have furniture and other belongings in storage somewhere?"

"No. I lived in the east wing of my parents' house. My things are still there."

East wing? Wow. How big is their house?

No wonder he had such a snooty air and attitude about him. People with *wings* on their houses usually had maids and cooks and people to do things for them. This led her back to questioning why he would rather live in her garage apartment than what sounded like a family mansion and with no doubt access to all the nannies he could want.

"You have no pots and pans or dishes or even a TV?"

"No. Guess I should've thought of that when we were at the store. For tonight, can I borrow a towel and a pillow and blanket?"

She wanted to laugh at his don't-you-think-I'm-adorable grin, but she did not want him to know that she was beginning to find him entertaining. "I suppose that can be arranged."

"Thanks. Does Oak Hollow have more than one pizza delivery? I tried one of the chain restaurants while I was at the hotel, but I wasn't impressed."

"Yes. There are two options. Want to see the menu for the one I like best?"

"Please. I'm suddenly starving again."

She grabbed a menu from a kitchen drawer and handed it to him. "The Mediterranean Greek pizza is really good."

"Works for me. I love Greek food. Sara makes wonderful spanakopita and stuffed grape leaves."

"Who is Sara?" she asked and started putting away clean dishes from the drain rack.

"The chef and house manager at Weller Estate. She's been with our family for almost thirty years."

Unable to keep her eyes from going wide, she turned so he couldn't see her face. Just as she'd suspected, he was used to special treatment. "You've never had to cook for yourself?"

"Not really. I used to help Sara make cookies at Christmastime. And I can make a great sandwich."

"You do know that the baby lessons do not include me cooking for you, right? And the apartment does not come with maid service."

"Yes. I am capable of learning and doing things for myself, and I'm aware of how the real world works. I'm asking enough from you already."

That was certainly the truth, especially considering her plan to pamper herself for at least a week had been put on the back burner.

He made the call and ordered pizza while she finished tidying the kitchen.

"Let's unpack some of these purchases, and while we wait for dinner, I'll teach you how to sterilize the baby bottles." She pushed the large baby swing box his way and started taking tags off new clothes.

"Should I be writing stuff down?"

"Not a bad idea."

Nicholas opened a music app on his cell phone and the room filled with the catchy beat of the Ed Sheeran song "Shivers." Although tempted to break into a full-body dance, Emma didn't know this guy well enough to be that uninhibited in front of him. But it was impossible to keep her body from swaying as she moved around the house. When she thought she heard him chuckle, she glanced over her shoulder and caught him with a smile that appeared genuine. Not the hard-to-read fake one she usually saw.

It surprised her that in the time it took her to re-move tags from the new baby clothes, start a load of laundry and put the bottles by the sink, he had the swing assembled and had unboxed the Diaper Genie.

Lifting the lid, he peered inside. "I was hoping a genie would pop out and grant my wish to change the dirty diapers, but no such luck."

"Some wishes are harder to grant than others." And other wishes were completely impossible, but even so, hope and light were coming back into her life a little more with each day. Maybe this experience would turn out to be good for her.

They shared pizza and salad while comparing childhood experiences. Then after another feeding and diapering, she gathered towels, bedding and a few other things he might need for the night.

"Be a good boy for Emma." He kissed his son on the top of his head and grabbed the borrowed items but paused to look at her before going out the door. "You are a lifesaver. I'll see you in the morning."

"See you then. Good night."

She closed the door behind him and flipped on the outdoor light. He moved quickly across the yard, long shadows trailing him up the white wooden stair-case.

While Nicholas had been with her, asking ques-tions and needing her support, there had been enough distraction to keep from acknowledging the fact that she was taking care of a baby for the first time in years. The quiet of the house settled over her, but only for a moment before Jax cried from his bassinet. She was alone in her home…with a baby. A baby who wasn't hers and never would be.

The ache that was always present on some level kicked up a notch. As much as she tried to keep her mind focused on the present, emotional memories crept in. She held Jax cradled on one shoulder. He nuzzled his face against her and then quieted as she stood in front of her wedding photo. Although it had been way too short, she'd had the perfect marriage and didn't expect to ever be so lucky again. Any other guy would only disappoint her, never living up to Steven. Her ruggedly handsome husband had been the love of her life since high school. Steven had never owned designer clothes or driven an impractical car. As a game warden, he'd worn jeans, boots and soft flannel in the wintertime. So very different from Nicholas Weller.

She adjusted the porcelain rabbit on the fireplace mantel, remembering the Christmas Steven gave it to her, long before they were married. Back when he'd given her the nickname Bunny Rabbit after one hopped up beside her on a picnic in the woods.

"I know what you would say. Jump back into life and stop wasting time I could be using to make happy memories. You were always so positive. Finding something good in even the worst situation." She patted the baby's back and took comfort in the feel of him in her arms. "But without you, doing that has been really hard. I miss you so much, Steven. Kiss our baby girl and hold her tight." She blew a kiss to the photo and turned away before tears started.

Once she'd made the last bottle before bedtime, Emma made her way down the darkened hallway and stood outside her daughter's nursery. The one Rose had never had the chance to sleep in. Her hand trembled as she reached for the doorknob, but she could not make herself open it.

More than one person had suggested she pack everything away until she needed it again, but she just couldn't make herself dismantle the room she'd worked so hard on. She used to sit in the room for hours and cry for the family she'd lost when a truck driver made the fatal decision to text while driving, but she rarely even opened the door anymore. Still, she could picture the room in her mind. Every precious detail of the handmade bunny rabbit mobile and curving lines of the refinished antique bookcase. There was a great rocking chair in there, but in the end, she couldn't make herself go inside with a baby who wasn't her Rose.

Emma turned for her room, sat on the edge of her bed and sang until Jax fell asleep. She put him in the bassinet beside her bed, but rather than taking a shower, she watched him sleep with one fist tucked against his smooth cheek. He was adorable, and if today was an indication, he was a good-natured, happy baby.

"Sweet dreams until sunbeams find you."

Could I have a baby on my own? Be a single parent like Nicholas will be?

Until this moment, that was a possibility she hadn't let herself think about.

When weariness crept into her body, she took a shower, then settled into bed with a book, but after one page her eyes were drifting closed. With one more peek at the sleeping baby and a gentle kiss to his head, she let her mind and body rest.

Jax only woke once in the night and then again at six thirty in the morning.

His father, however, did not wake up at six thirty or seven thirty or even eight thirty. Nicholas finally knocked on her back door at 9:00 a.m.

"Is the baby awake?" he asked.

A deep calming breath did little to ease her frustration or make up for her lack of sleep. "He's been awake for two and a half hours and just gone back to sleep."

"Oh. Sorry." He hooked his thumbs in the front pockets of a pair of dark-wash jeans. "I usually wake up earlier, but as you can probably imagine, I had trouble getting to sleep last night. I've got a lot of new things on my mind."

Emma couldn't help but notice he'd taken the time

to style his hair, while she was sporting a messy ponytail and no makeup. At least he was wearing casual clothes today. His dark green T-shirt was hugging the impressive pecs and biceps she'd gotten a peek at when he'd taken off his wet shirt. And while his jeans were designer instead of her preferred Levi's or Wranglers, they fit just right.

Stop staring at him!

"Your son will be your alarm clock tomorrow morning. Want some coffee?"

"Yes, please. I need to add a coffee maker to my growing shopping list." He glanced around the kitchen. "Where is Jax?"

"He's having a morning nap in his bassinet in the living room. Lucky for you, you can have coffee before changing your first diaper of the day." He groaned, and she grinned behind the rim of her coffee mug. "There are bagels by the toaster if you're hungry."

He filled her large #1 Teacher mug and took a sip of black coffee. "I'm really racking up the favors. I'm going to owe you big-time."

"Never fear. I'm keeping track." Sipping her own coffee, she winked like he'd done to her a time or two, and he chuckled. "So, yesterday you learned how to hold a baby, make a bottle, install the car seat and change a diaper… Sort of."

"Why do you think I wore a T-shirt and jeans today, just in case of surprise accidents or projectile messes." He plucked the fabric of his shirt away from his flat belly. "These are clothes that don't have to be dry-cleaned."

"That reminds me, I washed your shirt that the baby peed on yesterday."

His coffee mug paused on the way to his mouth. "You washed it? Like in a washing machine?"

Her eyes rolled before she could stop them. "Well, I didn't use a washboard at the river."

"But…" He blinked a few times. "I dry-clean my button-up shirts."

When both of her eyebrows rose, he sighed. Every time she started to believe he wasn't so high main-tenance or unlike the other men she knew, he did or said something that reminded her how different he was. "It didn't say dry-clean only, and it's not ruined. I hung it up to dry."

"I have other shirts. It's fine," he said.

"You don't know how to iron, do you?" She grinned when he ducked his head and shoved a hand into his back pocket.

"Can't say that I do."

"I have a steamer at the shop, and I'll teach you how to use it. It will take the wrinkles right out. And for the baby's sake, I'll teach you how to use a washer and dryer, too."

"Probably a good idea. What's on today's lesson plan, teacher?"

The heated look he shot her way made something

flutter in her stomach, and she did not like it. Liking this guy was not on the advised-activity list.

"Giving him a bath, for one thing. And other than that, let's start with your questions and that will tell me what areas are most important to hit first."

"Um…"

He scratched his smooth cheek, telling her he'd also taken the time to shave before coming downstairs. How did he manage to look so handsome without a full night's sleep? Tomorrow morning was going to be a different story.

"I guess I need to know what kind of schedule I should make. A schedule is always a good idea."

She'd bet becoming a father in a matter of minutes had thrown a massive wrench into *his* normal schedule. "I'll get a spiral notebook. It can become your parenting handbook." They went over a few baby-related things and finished their coffee before Jax woke up.

"All right, Daddy, you're up for a diaper change and then a bottle." Embarrassment slapped her.

Oh my God. Why in the hell did I call him Daddy? Maybe he didn't notice.

The grin he was attempting to hide suggested he had most definitely heard her, because she knew he wasn't smiling about the prospect of changing a diaper. The diapering went off without much trouble, and with a fresh bottle in hand, he headed for the high-back chair across from the couch.

"Did you remember to test the formula to make sure it's not too hot?"

Nicholas squirted some into his mouth and made a face as he shivered. "That's awful. How can he drink this stuff?" He glared at the bottle as if it had committed a great offense.

Her morning's annoyance faded a bit more. At least the man was entertaining and made her laugh. "Remember how I tested it on the inside of my wrist? Try that next time. And don't worry about Jax. He doesn't have taste buds as developed as ours yet."

"Thank God. I'd hate to think I'm torturing my child with this every time he eats." Jax waved a fist and let out a little squawk. Nicholas settled into the chair and brushed the nipple against the baby's mouth. Jax reached out with both tiny hands, clasping one on the bottle and one around his father's fingers. "I'm glad you like it, little man."

The touching moment warmed her. It was a beautiful thing to see him bonding with his baby. Nicholas looked at her with the happiest expression she'd seen from him yet. She'd thought his white teeth were perfectly straight, but now that she was witnessing an authentic smile, there was a top tooth on one side that tilted just the slightest but enough to let her know he wasn't a perfect Ken doll.

"How am I doing, teacher? Do I get a passing grade for today?"

"Yes. You're doing great. A solid B-plus," she said with a teasing smile.

"Well, that leaves room for improvement."

Not so long ago, she'd found Nicholas annoying and hoped he would leave town, but the cocky bachelor was becoming someone she wanted to know.

Chapter Five

On the day they found Jax, Nicholas had been something close to terrified he'd break his baby boy, or at the least do something majorly wrong and embarrass himself, but midway through his first full day of lessons, he was only mildly frightened. Afternoon sunlight streamed in the western windows, and he brushed the curve of his son's cheek. Jax's lips drew up like a bow and sucked on an imaginary bottle in his sleep.

"You are pretty amazing, little man." This tiny creature had stolen his heart and there was no going back. This new feeling, although terrifying, was too incredible to even think about giving up.

He stood ever so carefully from the living room chair and held his breath while placing Jax in the bassinet. With too much nervous energy to be still, he walked around Emma's living room and stopped in front of an old cabinet record player. The wooden top was open, revealing the turntable and a collection of albums. Amazing how you used to need a piece of furniture and large vinyl discs to enjoy music and now you only needed a smartphone. But the old way was so much cooler.

Emma came in the front door with fresh flowers she'd cut from her rosebushes and kicked her blue flip-flops under the front-door bench.

"Does this record player work?" he asked.

"Yes. I use it all the time. It belonged to my grandparents, as did this house." Emma set down the roses and crossed the room to pull out a record and put it on at a low volume. "At Last" by Etta James began playing. "I used to watch my grandparents dance to this song. My grandfather would sing along as he spun her around the living room."

"Does your..." Nicholas pressed his lips together. Asking about her husband was a bad idea. Since there had been no mention of him, he knew it couldn't be good.

She followed his gaze to her wedding photo above the fireplace. "My husband, Steven. He couldn't carry a tune, but he was a good dancer. It's been almost four years since I lost him."

Her husband died, too? She lost her whole family?

His face was no doubt broadcasting his thoughts, so he glanced to the side until he got control. "I'm sorry you had to go through that." Moving to the sofa, he sat facing her, so she'd know he was willing to listen. Really listen.

"Sometimes I still find myself turning to tell him something." She shook her head as if trying to dislodge a memory. "While the baby is napping, let's get the paint and other supplies out of the garage, and you can start on your side of this deal. I can watch Jax while you work."

And that seemed to be her way of saying they weren't going to talk any more about her husband. "I'll go change into my old work clothes."

One of her eyebrows arched. "You have those?"

"Yes. I wear them when I work on my car."

"Hmm. You continue to surprise me, Nicholas Weller."

"In good ways, I hope?" *Does she really believe I'm that much of a pampered snob? Am I?*

"Mostly good," she said and softened her answer with a full grin. "How many days do you think it will take to paint the whole garage? I told Jenny I'd come in to work on Monday."

Which meant he got one more full day of lessons tomorrow and would then be on his own on Monday. "Since the garage is two-story, it will probably take three whole days, at least. It will depend on how many hours I have each time I paint."

"There's really no set timeline for having it done," she said.

"I forgot to ask how much the rent is for the apartment."

For a few seconds she just stared at him. "You want to rent it for real? Not just stay there temporarily?"

"If you'll let me." *Does she not want me here?* "It will allow me to take my time looking for something larger." But did he really need anything bigger? He wasn't staying in Oak Hollow permanently and being close to Emma was suddenly an appealing option.

"Okay. That makes sense. It's so small that I was only charging seven hundred a month before the renovation."

He could almost see the wheels turning in her head but couldn't guess what she was thinking. "How does one thousand a month sound?"

"Sounds like I should give you the rental paperwork."

"Great. I'll go change my clothes and meet you outside."

When he came back downstairs wearing his faded grease-stained jeans and a black T-shirt he saved for working on his car, she was in the garage. The space was organized into sections for tools, garden-

ing and painting supplies, camping gear and a place
to work out.

Emma was making so much noise trying to pull
an extension ladder from behind a stack of plastic
crates that she didn't hear him come up behind her.
She gave the ladder another shake and growled when
it didn't come free.

"Come on, you stupid freaking hunk of junk."

Nicholas almost laughed at her creative exple-
tive but laughing at an angry woman was never a
good idea. His mother and sister had taught him that
lesson. Although he found Emma fascinating and
wanted to see what she'd say next, he could see that
the ladder was caught on the corner of a metal shelf.
He stepped forward to help her right as she stomped
her foot, spun around and collided with him, her
open palms slapping against his chest. Catching her
by the shoulders, he kept them both upright.

Time took a brief pause as they stared at one another, and something passed between them. Something heated and full of electrically charged tension
he really wanted to explore. When a flash of interest
crossed her face, and she grasped the fabric of his
T-shirt, he fought the urge to pull her in closer and
discover the taste of her lips.

"Need help?" he asked.

As if his voice broke the spell, she sucked in a
breath, let go of his shirt and then stepped to the
other side of a wheelbarrow like she needed a bar-

rier between them. "I hate to admit it, but I do. The damn thing is stuck." She narrowed her eyes and shot a glare at the offending bit of metal.

He covered his urge to laugh with unnecessary throat clearing, then with a lift and twist, he maneuvered it free and carried it outside.

"You're lucky," she said and followed him with a five-gallon container of white paint.

"I am?" Where was she going with this? Because the first place his mind went was getting lucky with her.

"Yes. The wood has already been sanded and prepped for painting. You get the easy part."

Well, that's boring. "Lucky me."

"If you need me, I'll be inside with the baby," she said and almost tripped over a potted plant as she rushed for her back door.

Need her? His body heated further. Currently, need and want were swirled together in a confusing jumble. And if he wasn't mistaken, it wasn't only his imagination, there was electricity sparking between them. But Emma was fighting it.

Nicholas set up the extension ladder on the side of the garage that faced the backyard, opened the container of white paint and stirred it before pouring some into a tray. The wet paint glistened in the sunlight like Emma's lips when she'd nervously licked them before dashing inside. And with every stroke of the brush, his imagination painted a fantasy life. What would it be like to be with a woman like Emma?

A couple of hours later, Emma came outside with Jax and set him on the center of a blanket in the shade. "You're making good progress."

With one arm braced on the top of the ladder, he smiled down at her. "It will go even faster when I get to the lower part and don't have to keep moving the ladder and going up and down."

"No doubt." She started weeding the flower bed next to where the baby chewed on his toy giraffe.

They worked in companionable silence, with undertones of sexual tension hanging in the humid summer air. When he finished the side that faced the backyard, he stood back and looked at the blank canvas. Fresh and clean but boring. It was calling out for something more interesting. Maybe a mural.

Emma came up beside him. "Very nice work."

"Thanks. What do you think about putting a mural on this one side of the garage? You'd only see it if you are in the backyard."

"I've never thought of that. My friend Alexandra is an artist, and she has painted a couple of murals around town."

"I could paint one," Nicholas said then rubbed the back of his neck. *More like I wish I could do something like that.*

She looked him over much like he'd surveyed the wall. "You can paint a mural? When you said you could paint, I didn't think you meant you were an artist."

"I'm not, but I've always wanted to be."

She sat beside the baby and lifted him into her arms. "You work with art and should have the opportunity to create it."

He shrugged, not wanting to go into the details about his family's expectations or that his parents had actively discouraged him from pursuing art. He was only supposed to sell it. "I've just been busy with other things."

By that night, Nicholas had painted one side of the garage, learned to give a slippery, squirming baby a bath and dress him, and had a long conversation with a lawyer about DNA tests, birth certificates and loads of legal paperwork. He'd also called the pediatrician in Houston and was happy to hear that Jax was in excellent health. His medical records were being transferred to the local doctor Emma had suggested. Now, he was truly exhausted in a way he hadn't been since the time he ran a marathon.

Jax made cute baby noises and threw his rattle, reminding Nicholas that he was alone in his mostly empty apartment with his son…who was depending on him for everything.

Every. Single. Thing.

Nicholas sat on the edge of the tan sofa and dropped his head into his hands. "How am I supposed to finish the renovations, curate inventory and open a business while I'm learning how to take care of you?"

Monday he would meet with his contractor to discuss the final stage of the gallery restoration. He was working with Philip Deco to combine a Deco Vineyard wine-tasting room with his gallery. A mounting list of important things that needed doing, and the gigantic cherry on top—and most important of all—was learning to be a father to his son.

Jax tossed his giraffe rattle, then rolled to his side but couldn't reach it.

Retrieving the toy, Nicholas sat beside the baby blanket where his son played. "Here you go, little man. I'll make your bottle in a few minutes."

He'd yet to tell anyone about his sudden fatherhood, because if he told anyone who knew his parents it could get back to them before he was ready. Before he knew how to break this unexpected epic news. He could almost see the judgmental expression on his mother's face and hear his father's stern voice disapproving of the manner in which Nicholas had become a father. First, he needed to make progress on the art gallery, and once he had something good to report, he would think about contacting his parents.

An old familiar knot settled in his gut, heavy and oily with a feeling of inadequacy. It had been years since this sensation had made an appearance. Probably since he was a teenager. And he did not like it.

"I'm too old for this crap. No thirty-five-year-old man should be feeling teenage insecurities." He rubbed his hands over his face, inhaled deeply and then patted his son's tummy. "I will never make you think your best isn't good enough." Hauling himself up off the floor, he went into the kitchen to make a bottle.

A little later, Nicholas attempted to sleep on the couch folded out into a bed, but because it was like sleeping on old car parts, he gave up on that idea and folded it up again. He had no sooner fallen asleep on the couch that was way too short for his six-foot-two frame, when Jax woke up crying in the frantic way that made his tongue quiver between his bare gums. He did all the things Emma had taught him to do. Gave him a fresh diaper. Made a bottle and tested it to make sure it wasn't too hot, and this time he did that on his wrist and not by squirting the awful stuff into his mouth. Feeding, burping, walking and singing. After the longest hour of his adult life, his baby was finally asleep. Nicholas fell onto the couch and slept while he could.

Sunday morning, Jax was his alarm clock, just like Emma had promised. And unfortunately, he still didn't have a coffee maker. Just when he was about to go begging at Emma's door, someone knocked on his. With Jax tucked in the crook of one arm, he answered to find Emma with a cup of hot, black coffee.

"Good morning," she said, and her full lips lifted into a sweet smile.

"You are a lifesaver. Again." As she gave him the coffee and took the baby from him, he caught the scent of peaches from her hair as it curtained down around her face. His pulse jumped and sped in a new way.

Emma lifted Jax to her eye level, and he grabbed for her hair. "Good morning, sweetie." As hard as she tried to resist, falling for this precious baby was unavoidable. "Were you a good boy for your daddy?"

"I think we did pretty good for our first night alone together."

"Excellent. Since you don't have any food in your apartment yet, would you like to come have breakfast downstairs?" Even though she'd told him she would not be cooking for him, it was nice to have someone to feed because cooking for one was no fun.

"That would be great."

She started down the stairs with Jax, and Nicholas followed, still barefoot and wearing a T-shirt and a pair of running shorts she kind of loved. They showed off his runner's legs, long and leanly muscled.

"We can go to the grocery store later," she said.

"And I'm willing to bet you haven't spent much time in one."

"You might be right, but I'll never tell." He closed her back door behind them and moved close enough to drop a kiss on his son's head.

His nearness made her stomach do some kind of hula dance. Having Nicholas around wasn't as unpleasant as she'd thought it would be. He smelled really good, like warm spices, and with his cocky smile wiped away by the business of becoming a father, he was…tolerable. Okay, more than tolerable.

After they had eaten, they started on the day's baby lessons. Emma put Jax on his tummy in the center of a blanket in the sunny spot under the windows where she had envisioned a play area. The baby's legs churned behind him like he was running a race as he babbled against his hands.

Nicholas lowered to his stomach on eye level with his son. "He's strong, right? For a baby his age?"

The way Nicholas smiled at his son warmed Emma's heart. "Yes, he is. Did you make his doctor's appointment?"

"I did, and I got the records transferred. They said he's healthy."

"His uncle Marco took good care of him."

"I called Marco yesterday, and he's all moved in with his friends in Austin."

"That's good. He did the right thing bringing Jax to you. He deserves to be a college kid."

"I remember that time in my life," he said.

His voice was so quiet she thought maybe he was talking only to himself. "What's next on the lesson plan?" she asked, knowing full well what it was.

Propping up on one elbow, he glanced at the crumpled bullet-point list. "Taking a baby's temperature."

She had been playing with the idea of teasing him about how to do this task, and because he had a playful teasing side, she was going for it. She held up a slender old-style thermometer with a little flourish of her wrist. "You need to lubricate this with the Vaseline and then very carefully insert it."

"That doesn't sound right." His head cocked to one side, and he ran his tongue across his front teeth. "It can't be good to get Vaseline in his mouth?"

"Not in his mouth." Emma patted the baby's bottom and bit her cheek to keep from laughing.

Nicholas gasped so hard he coughed, then sat up. "You can't be serious."

His horrified reaction was even better than she'd hoped, and she laughed so hard she snorted, which made her fit of giggles continue until he joined in. "Sorry. I couldn't resist messing with you."

"You are a mean, wicked woman, Emma Blake," he said, but chuckled again.

It took a few more seconds to get herself under control enough to speak and get back to the business of baby lessons. "That used to be the way a baby's temp was taken, but now…" She held up a forehead-scanning thermometer. "Now we have this handy-dandy option." She leaned forward, put it to Nicholas's forehead and pushed the button.

"Do I have a fever, Dr. Emma?"

His wolfish grin kindled a wave of heat that started in her core. Was this what he did to all his women? The beautiful, glamorous ones she'd seen in photos when she couldn't resist checking him out on the internet? Most of the photos had been taken at fancy parties at his family's auction house, and it was a world she didn't know. Tempted to say he was giving *her* a fever, she resisted, not willing to feed his ego.

"Nope. You're normal. Most of the time." Needing some physical distance from him, she got to her feet. "I'm walking to the square to pick up a birthday present for a friend." Hopefully that would give her time to cool off. "We can pick up the lessons later."

"Can we come along? Unless you want me to stay here and paint."

"The painting can wait." *Why did I say that? So much for time to cool off. Time for plan B.* "It will be lunchtime soon and we can eat at the Acorn Café, and there are a few things I want to show you around town. Since I know you aren't going out in public in your current outfit, go change. I'll give Jax a fresh diaper and make a bottle and then we can get going."

With the baby in the stroller, they headed down her driveway. "Before we go to the square, I want to take a detour and show you something."

Jax had been lulled to sleep with the motion of them walking, and they spoke in hushed tones.

Nicholas looked at her funny when she went up the front walk of the old blue-and-white Craftsman-style house with a sign that read Queen's Sew N Sew.

"Are you taking me into a fabric store?"

"It's more than just a fabric store. You'll see."

With a skeptical noise in the back of his throat, he followed her inside. The front room of the old house was filled with brightly colored fabrics and had quilts displayed on the walls.

"Is that made out of fabric?" Nicholas drew close to a detailed quilt that looked like a painting.

Emma chuckled. "I told you a quilt can be art."

"Hmm. I stand corrected."

His willingness to admit when he was wrong was a refreshing thing. "Keep going this way and we'll see more."

When they passed by the back room, the Queen Mother's sewing club spotted them, and there was no getting away from this lovely group of grandmothers and great-grandmothers. Jax was an instant hit, and Nicholas turned on his sophisticated charm and spoke to all the women as she imagined he did with auction house clientele. The only difference was that he was wearing khaki pants and a casual button-up instead of a fancy Prada suit and tie.

There was no shortage of loaded questions about her and Nicholas's relationship status, but she instantly assured everyone that they were nothing more than friends. What she didn't add was that she was not looking for more than that. She wasn't ready for a romantic relationship and wasn't sure she ever would be. Staying unattached was safer. And when she caught a few glances of sympathy as the women looked between her and the baby, it reinforced her decision.

When Jax cried, several women insisted on holding him and before they left, Nicholas chose a quilt made by Nan Curry, the original queen mother. The quilt was made with brilliant jewel tones and a ton of talent.

Once they made it to the center of the square, their first stop was Hallie's jewelry store.

Nicholas held the door for her. "Is this another I-told-you-so mission to prove what is considered art?"

Emma smiled and went through the doorway with the stroller. "I'm picking up a pair of handmade earrings for a friend's birthday, but I certainly won't stop you if you happen to see something artistic."

"Very subtle," he said.

The way his lips twitched made other parts of her come alive. These kinds of feelings and tingles were so unexpected that she momentarily forgot what she was here for.

Nicholas commissioned a few pieces of jewelry for his gallery before they made their way to the Acorn Café. There was a line of people in front of the bakery case by the front register. It was filled with bread, cookies, pastries and the most irresistible cinnamon rolls. Thankfully there were open tables, and they chose one in the back of the restaurant so the stroller wouldn't be in the way of foot traffic.

"You should probably change his diaper before we eat," she said. "And before you say it, no, I'm not doing it. This is on the lesson plan. How to change a diaper while out in public."

"But aren't those fold-down changing tables in the women's restroom?"

His hopeful expression made her grin. "Good try, Nick. There are two one-person bathrooms that either sex can use, and they both have a changing station."

His smile faded. "No one ever calls me Nick."

"If it bothers you, I won't do it again." Taken aback by his statement, she flipped open her menu and held it up between them.

"No, I like it," he said. "It fits coming from you."

"Really?" She lowered the menu. "I'm not sure what that says about me, but okay."

He slung the diaper bag over his shoulder, lifted

his baby from the stroller and held her gaze. "It says, you get special privileges."

Special privileges?

He shot her an unreadable expression before walking away. One that made her feel sparkly inside and out. Did he mean only that she'd made it past the "hired help" status, or was he hinting at something... more personal? Doing her very best to ignore the feelings he stirred, she ordered drinks.

Nicholas returned looking slightly green.

"Was it that bad?" she asked and forced herself not to laugh.

"Yes, it was *that* bad."

She held out her arms and took the wide-awake and wiggling baby. "Did your daddy do a good job, sweetie? Does he get an A-plus?"

Jax waved his arms and cooed happily.

"That's a yes," Nicholas said and dropped back into his chair. "It's entirely possible I deserve an extra plus on that A."

The waitress brought their iced teas, cold and sweet and just what she needed on such a hot day. They placed their orders while several other diners tried to be stealthy about their observations.

"I have to admit that you are right about the local artists," Nicholas said. "You have turned this art snob into a believer."

"Wow. That fast?"

"I'm a quick study." He winked before guzzling his iced tea.

Rather than being put off by his wink like she had been, this time it was…charming. Kind of like he'd said about it feeling right for her to call him Nick. This old-fashioned expression was very Nick.

"Do you see the blond woman at the bakery case holding hands with the tall dark-haired guy? She is the nurse practitioner at the doctor's office where Jax has his appointment."

"I know him. That's Christopher Lopez. He's one of the guys working on the restoration of my gallery. They're married?"

"No. Just dating. But I suspect it has gotten serious between them." Emma pushed aside her empty plate. "I'm really glad you are restoring your retail space rather than remodeling it into some ultra-modern gallery that would be out of place in Oak Hollow."

"I've grown up in a business that sells a lot of antique pieces. I appreciate old things and styles."

"That's a good attitude to have around this historic town. What are you going to name your gallery?"

"I haven't decided yet, but probably something simple like The Weller Gallery & Tasting Room."

"Don't make it too long like we did. It's hard to fit on the sign," she chuckled.

"Maybe you can help me think of something shorter."

"I'll try. Maybe Weller's Art & Wine."

"That could work."

"Are you ready to go?"

"Ready."

Jax had finished a bottle that she'd made Nick give him while eating one-handed, and he was sleeping again.

Upon leaving the café, she once again spotted Gwen and Christopher in the gazebo. She was standing, and he suddenly dropped to one knee before her. Emma's breath caught painfully in her chest, and she abruptly stopped walking.

Christopher stood, and she realized he'd only been tying his shoe, but it had been enough to trigger a memory of Steven kneeling before her in that very same spot, his dark eyes shining like the diamond in his hand. She touched her ring and twisted it around her finger, much like her heart was twisting in her chest.

"Emma, what is it?" Nicholas put a hand on the center of her back.

"Nothing. I'm fine." She stepped away from his touch and continued walking toward home, not wanting to tell him that was the spot where Steven had proposed to her. The vivid memory of that happy time had thrown her and reminded her of what could happen.

The rest of their afternoon, she tried to keep her distance from the man who had tapped directly into her sex drive. She'd even offered to watch the baby and sent Nick to the grocery store so she would have some time to think without his scent distracting her. But it wasn't working.

Chapter Six

Nicholas was only halfway through the grocery store and three women had flirted with him. Ordinarily, he would be happy and probably would have gotten a phone number or two, but he hadn't even been tempted. While going up and down aisles of food he didn't know how to cook, all he could think about was Emma and the way she moved as if she was one step away from swaying into a graceful dance. The curve of her waist and hips. Her loving nature with Jax. The tilt of her beautiful eyes that reminded him of a cat, and forefront in his mind was a desire to make her purr with pleasure.

During their morning tour of the local art, the

mood between them had been easygoing with lots of joking and laughing. He'd even had fun at the fabric store—which was something he never thought would happen. But somewhere between the café and the florist shop, the vibe changed, and their connection dissolved like ice cubes in the Texas heat. One minute she'd seemed to be enjoying herself and the next Emma had shut down on him, but he wasn't sure why. If he'd done something offensive, he had no idea what it was.

Grabbing several boxes of breakfast cereal, he overheard a woman talking on her cell phone about her boyfriend not understanding women, and he felt like he could sympathize with the guy. Was he overreacting and looking for problems with Emma where there were none?

I wish someone would write a handbook about how to figure out the minds of women.

After buying the retail space on the square and having no paycheck coming in from the auction house, he couldn't throw money around like he used to. Most of his investments couldn't be touched for years yet, and saving money was something he needed to work on. He was a father now and had to be more serious about planning for the future.

Every item he put in his shopping cart was adding up at a rate he'd never had to think about before. A cheap set of dishes and silverware that would make his mother faint. A coffee maker, a toaster and food he'd have to figure out how to cook.

I'm shopping as if I'm setting up a long-term home. What am I going to do with all these things when I go back to Houston?

Suddenly, the thought of leaving Oak Hollow made him sad, and he needed to think long and hard about why that was.

On the drive back home, someone honked, and he pulled forward through the light that had turned green without him noticing. "I need to get my head out of the clouds. This is not the time to be distracted." But that was a tall order when Emma Blake had gotten under his skin. A few minutes later, he parked his Corvette beside her car and hauled his groceries and other purchases upstairs, then with one bag of items he'd picked up for Emma, he knocked on her back door.

"Come in," she called out.

"I got everything you asked for, and also some of those cookies you like."

"Thanks. Just set everything on the counter and I'll put it away," she said from the kitchen sink. "All the baby bottles are washed and packed in the diaper bag, and Jax is ready to go up to your apartment. I think we've had enough lessons for today." Giving the dish towel a quick snap, she hung it up. "I'm going to take a bath, read a book and go to bed early."

Her dismissal stung. "Okay. I appreciate your looking after Jax while I shopped."

"Sure."

He wasn't overreacting. Something was wrong and had changed between them. Just when they were getting close, she was pulling away. And the way she was biting her lip and twisting her wedding ring, he had a pretty good idea what it had to do with. Emma was still mourning her husband and perhaps feeling guilty about moving on. He needed to give her time.

"Don't forget that I'm going to my shop tomorrow morning," she said as she went into the living room, lifted the sleeping baby from his blanket and kissed his cheek. "But we can continue lessons in the afternoon."

"Sounds good. I also need to go to my gallery in the morning for a meeting with the contractor." Jax woke as he took him from her arms. "Hello, little man. Did you have a nice nap?"

"Make sure you pack everything Jax will need and also take the baby sling when you go to your meeting in the morning."

"Will do. Sleep well, Em." With his child held against his chest, he went out her back door and up to his lonely apartment.

With his refrigerator and pantry stocked and Jax having tummy time, he settled in for his second night as a single father. Supper was a TV dinner, and because he had no actual television, his entertainment was an audiobook played on his phone. He mentally prepared for diapering, feeding and putting his baby to bed followed by a shower and sleep. However, Jax was not fully on board with tonight's agenda.

When they should've both been asleep, Jax would not stop crying. With the baby in every position he could think of, they paced back and forth across the small space of the apartment. Nothing was working. Not a clean diaper or full tummy or time in the baby swing. He even resorted to reading an article in *Antiques & Fine Art* magazine like it was a bedtime story, but he only managed to bore himself.

Jax kicked his chubby legs and cried around his wet fist.

"Little man, what can I do to help you?"

Tempted to call Emma more times than he could count, he finally grabbed his phone from the kitchen counter but put it down immediately. Two minutes later, he picked it up again and pulled up her contact, but squeezed his eyes closed.

"No. I can do this on my own."

He dropped the phone onto the couch cushion. With the way Jax was screaming, he wouldn't have been able to hear her over the phone anyway. This was something he needed to do. To prove his ability not only to her but also to himself.

"Help me out here, kid. I really hate to see you so miserable. What's wrong?"

Jax arched, grunted and then stopped crying a few seconds later. And then came the odor.

"Oh, son." Nicholas covered his nose and rushed for the area he'd set up for diaper changing and the face mask he'd bought for just such occasions. "Well, I did ask you what was wrong."

Crying woke Nicholas at daybreak on Monday morning, and at first, he thought it was a dream. But only for a second. Without lifting his head, he reached into the bassinet to pat Jax. "Don't you want to go back to sleep, little man?"

It tickled when Jax gummed his finger, and Nicholas sat up. Staring down at his son's precious face, his exhaustion began to fade. He couldn't resist picking him up for a morning hug and enough kisses on his chubby cheeks to make him stop crying.

"You're lucky I finally bought a coffeepot. What do you say we go turn it on before we handle your diaper?" The baby stuck out his tongue as he stretched with a gummy grin. Nicholas couldn't help but laugh.

The day started out well enough, with the nutty aroma of coffee and a diaper that was a snap compared with last night's fiasco, but it escalated into chaos rather quickly. The rest of the morning routine included a spilled cup of coffee, burnt toast, two shaving nicks on Nicholas's chin and cheek and a couple of clothing changes for each of them.

He snapped on a green onesie and swaddled Jax.

"Maybe I should hire a real nanny. One whose sole job is to look after you while I'm working. Not to teach me what to do." He had Emma for that. She was showing him how to be the kind of parent who played ball with his son and was called "Daddy" rather than "Father."

"Wait… I can't hire a daytime nanny."

That would give Emma a reason to end their agreement, and that was unacceptable. He wanted their baby lessons to extend into another week and beyond. The judgy schoolteacher had charmed him and revealed herself to be an amazing and complicated woman. She was still healing from a tragedy he couldn't imagine. She needed someone who would listen and not push, and he'd give her that time. But he didn't want to give up on a chance to be more to her than the helpless guy who needed baby lessons. Emma was the kind of woman a man waited for. If she wanted him to go away, she would have to specifically tell him to leave.

But will she ever be ready or interested in being with someone like me? Am I wasting my time?

Finally, the diaper bag was packed, the carrier sling was stowed in the pocket of the stroller and they both had on clean clothes. He hadn't even considered grabbing a suit or dress shirt. Although his maroon T-shirt did have a designer label, it was machine washable and much more suited to his current situation. He took the stroller down the apartment stairs. One more trip up to collect the baby and they were ready for a walk to the town square.

He put the pacifier next to Jax just in case. "Time to go to work with your daddy, little man. We have a lot to get done today."

Jax popped a thumb into his mouth and his big curious eyes gave the impression he was very interested in what his daddy had to say.

"I hope your attention means that we have an understanding about how today should go. Agreed?"

"Does he agree?"

Nicholas started at the sound of Emma's voice from behind him but turned to her with a smile. "The jury is still out on that. Are you walking with us?"

"Sure. Just let me grab my purse."

Hopefully her willingness to be around him meant they could go back to being friends. *Give her time. Don't push.*

She was back a minute later, and they started down the shady driveway. A large leaf blew into the stroller, and Jax gave an excited squeal that sounded a lot like a giggle.

"Did you hear that?" he asked. "Did he laugh?"

Emma's smile made her eyes shine. "I think he did." She twirled the leaf above the baby, and they were rewarded with another giggle. Five minutes later, they set off again.

"Are you feeling better this morning?" he asked her.

She stared at her feet as they walked. "I was just tired. I'm good. I imagine I got more sleep than you."

"No doubt about that."

A pair of blue jays chased one another through the air and landed in a tree, and the scent of baked goods from the café carried on the warm breeze. From across the square, he saw Emma's business partner outside their shop with his construction contractor, Eric McKnight. She was petite, but he was taller than average and built like a linebacker with dark hair pulled back in a low ponytail. Jenny stood on her tiptoes to kiss him then went inside the dress shop.

"Jenny and Eric are a couple?"

"Yes, they're married. I thought you knew that. Aren't they cute together?"

"Sure. I guess so." *Do we look like a couple walking down the street with our baby?* If he asked that question aloud, she'd probably put even more distance between them. He once again reminded himself to give her time.

As they neared their shops, Eric was looking at his phone with his back and the sole of one boot against the wall beside Nicholas's gallery door. He glanced up and pushed away from the wall. "Morning."

"Good morning," Nicholas said.

"Eric, thanks for repairing the door to my office," Emma said and then put a hand on Nicholas's arm but seemed to realize what she'd done and jerked it away. "Just come over when you're ready to make a bottle."

"I will." The heat of her touch still lingered on his skin, and he wanted to follow her into her shop, but he could do this parenting thing all on his own.

And I'll just keep telling myself that.

When he turned his attention to unlocking his door, Eric wore a knowing grin.

Is my growing attraction that obvious?

"I brought the paint samples we talked about over the phone," the other man said.

"Excellent. Let's have a look at them."

Jax had been lulled to sleep by the motion of their walk, so Nicholas eased the stroller over the threshold as not to wake him.

"You've got a good-looking kid," Eric said and placed a stack of paint chips on top of the built-in display cabinet. "I heard about your sudden fatherhood situation, and I'm only saying something because I understand. I'm happy to lend an ear anytime."

"I appreciate that." Nicholas could certainly use another friend in town, and this was a welcomed offer. He could talk to Emma about some things but having another man's perspective would be a good idea.

"Seems like yesterday that my little girl was that tiny. She was premature and only weighed four and a half pounds when she was born."

"Wow, that's tiny."

"I was a single father for years. Until Jenny came into our lives." Eric glanced toward the wall that separated the gallery from the dress shop next door as if hoping he could catch a glimpse of his wife. "You're lucky to have Emma helping you from the very beginning."

"I one hundred percent agree with that. I'm honestly still in a bit of shock and disbelief. New town, new business and, surprise, a new baby."

"You've come to the right town. I'm from a big city, and Oak Hollow took some getting used to, but now I'm thankful for the closeness of this group of small-town friends." He fanned out the color choices, separating paint from stain options. "Choose your favorites and then we can narrow it down from there."

Nicholas stepped up for a closer look, but his mind was still turning over what the other man had said about this town. His original plan had been to get in and out of Oak Hollow as fast as he could, but now… He wasn't feeling any rush. And he didn't have to think about it twice to know who had a whole lot to do with that.

Am I falling for Emma because she is helping me or because she is…amazing?

"Did you know Emma's husband?"

"No. But I've heard that he was a good guy. He was a game warden. A dangerous job."

"That's how he died?"

"No. It was a car accident."

That must be why Emma is so concerned with the safety of my sports car.

When Emma entered the art gallery, Nicholas was wearing the baby in the blue-and-gray body sling and shaking hands with a beautiful, tall, willowy-thin woman she didn't know. The redhead was not anyone she'd ever seen around town, and the handshake seemed to linger a bit longer than necessary.

Prickles of jealousy crept over Emma like a wool blanket on a sweltering summer day, and it was a most uncomfortable feeling. This was the exact opposite of the plan to protect herself from future pain.

I cannot encourage his flirtation!

"It's been a real pleasure meeting you and your son. He is absolutely adorable," the other woman said and picked up a large black leather portfolio. "I'll call you."

"Thank you. I look forward to your call."

Emma smiled at her as she passed by on her way to the door. It wasn't the other woman's fault that she was having feelings that needed to be...forgotten.

Nicholas loosened the sling, shifted Jax into a cradled position and then took the bottle Emma held out. "Thanks for bringing this over. How did you know I was about to come make one?"

"Because I helped you make the schedule. Hello, sweet baby," she said to Jax and brushed the back of her fingers over his cheek. "Who was that lady?" She could've smacked herself for asking. It was none of her business. Nothing he did was any of her business, except maybe taking care of the baby. And that was only temporary.

"She's a sculptor from Austin."

"Are you getting any artwork from her?"

"Yes, I'm going to start with two of her pieces."

Emma took a seat on the office chair he'd moved up front to work on his laptop at the makeshift plywood table. The sound of hammering echoed from the bathroom area of the gallery. "If there's too much construction going on and it's not safe for Jax, bring him over to me."

"Thanks. I will. I don't want him in the same room with any of the construction."

She noticed a few sketches and doodles he'd drawn on a piece of paper. "You have an art history degree, you curate and sell art, but even though you want to create it, you don't. Tell me more about why that is."

"There was a time that I tried. I even managed to talk my parents into letting me take a painting class, but I wasn't very good at it."

"Very few people are good at something when they first start learning about it. As a teacher, I can tell you this is true. I always tell my students to keep trying and give it their best."

With a shrug, he patted his son with one hand and adjusted the bottle with the other. "That's good advice, in some cases. My parents thought it was a waste of time. I remember my father saying 'Son, there are more than enough artists and craftsmen out there, and you are needed at Weller's.' My time was better spent working at the auction house. Learning the ins and outs of the family business. Their plans for me did not include encouraging my personal artistic aspirations. Oh, and my mother decided my time would be better spent taking ballroom dancing lessons instead of art classes."

"Really? Why?"

"She said the skill was expected of a Weller at the parties and galas that are part of our clientele's community."

"Isn't that your community, too? The world you grew up in?"

"I suppose it is, but I've never fit nicely into their little boxes as they feel I should. Much to my parents' chagrin and frustration, I didn't always fall in line with their rules like my sister did. I used to wonder if I was switched with another baby at the hospital."

She tilted her head and looked him up and down. In casual clothing that better showed off his toned body than the fancy ones, and with a baby cradled against his chest, he was a delightful mixture of tender and tough and sexy. He was becoming someone new in her eyes. So different from the Nicholas Weller she'd first met and judged too harshly. His layer of cockiness was fading and only briefly making an appearance now and then. He was funny and could handle her teasing.

"What is it?" he asked and returned her inquisitive inspection. "Do I have something on my face?"

"No. I'm trying to picture you dancing the tango," she said to cover her intrusive observation.

He chuckled and shifted Jax to his shoulder to burp him. "That's not one of the dances I learned. Not much call for the tango at the parties I attend." He shook his head. "That I attended."

His saying "attended" in the past tense made it sound like he was done with that part of his life. As if he did not plan to go back to that world of galas and other elaborate events. And from the things he'd said about his parents, she couldn't blame him. "Do you miss the fancy parties? There's probably amazing food at some of them."

"No. I really don't. I'd rather eat at the Acorn Café." He rolled his head, and his neck cracked. "But I do miss my walk-in shower with the power jets. The couch is doing a number on my back. I also miss my good mattress. I can't put off buying one for much longer."

She had a great king-size mattress in her guest bedroom, but it would be impossible to fit it into the miniscule bedroom in the apartment. And having him sleep inside her house… That was an exciting but terrible idea. Getting to her feet, she adjusted the tie at the waist of her pink wraparound dress. "I better get back to my shop. I have a few things I need to do before I head home."

"I'm going to go back to my apartment now. Everything else I need to do can be done from my laptop. And Eric has a key to lock up when he's done."

"Okay. I'll see you later." She resisted the urge to cross the room and kiss the baby, because then she would also catch the scent of Nicholas's spicy aftershave and have to fight her desire to kiss him as well. Instead, she went back to her shop.

While Emma attempted to work, her thoughts battled like two feral cats in an alley. Push Nick away. Let Nick in. Give him a chance. Don't even consider it. She busied her hands straightening a rack of Jenny's fancier dress designs, but her mind would not cooperate and focus on business or fashion. Nick was not the stuck-up, snooty man she'd thought, but when would he realize he'd had enough of small-town life and go back to Houston? How long before he missed his world of glamour and wealth?

"Excuse me," said their new employee, Susan. "Since there aren't any customers right now, is it okay if I take my lunch break?"

"Sure. Are you going out to eat?"

"I brought my lunch. It's in the refrigerator. So, if you need my help just give me a shout."

"I'll be fine. Enjoy your lunch. And thank you for being so eager to learn. You are doing a great job helping customers."

"Thanks." The young girl beamed with a pleased grin and went into the back.

Focusing on the box of vintage clothes one of their longtime contacts had bought at an estate sale, Emma pulled out a red pencil skirt that she wanted for herself but would resist. At least going through new inventory was helping to keep her mind occupied. A vintage necklace with green glass jewels and rose gold leaves was tucked inside a small silver cardboard box.

"This is beautiful." Light glinted off the stones and made her think of her grandmother, who would've loved this necklace. When her contact had told her there was a nice piece of jewelry in the lot, she had trusted her but hadn't expected it to be this valuable. It was a perfect accessory for the chiffon dress they'd just put in the display window. Emma flashed back to being a little girl and helping Grams in the shop and at estate sales. So many wonderful memories, and it made her once again consider resigning from her teaching job to focus on what she loved most.

The joy of working in the shop where she'd grown up was occupying her mind and soothing her, until she reached the bottom of the box. A chocolate brown men's suit, which of course made her think of Nick, looked like a size that would probably fit him.

Oh, man. I've got it bad.

She grabbed a purple silk scarf from the box, took it to the display window to the left of the door and tied it around a mannequin's neck. She glanced up just as Nicholas and Jax walked past her shop window. He paused long enough to lift his son's arm for a wave and smiled in a way that made a swarm of butterflies flit about in her stomach. She watched until they were out of sight, then tried to concentrate on her work once again, but she ended up standing behind the front register with her elbows propped on the counter and her chin on her fists.

More and more of the things he did and said were adding up to his being a good guy. And since he was making a home for himself and Jax in Oak Hollow, could she…or rather *should* she even consider anything more than a friendship with him? Maybe they could ease into something casual. Something more than friends but not a serious relationship. Emma's stomach swirled and clenched.

I'm letting myself jump too far ahead. It's way too soon to even be considering something like having a relationship with a man I barely know.

Besides, what if part of her attraction to Nicholas was mostly because of his adorable baby who had stolen her heart? A child who needed a mother. The moment she thought it, she knew that wasn't true. Nicholas had captured her attention all on his own.

That evening, Emma stood at her stove making spaghetti while Nicholas gave the baby a bottle. Once he'd put Jax in his bassinet, he came into the kitchen and sat at the table.

"Is Jax asleep?"

"Yes. I'm getting pretty good at this parenting thing. For a beginner," he said with a crooked grin.

She couldn't resist teasing him. "I suppose you are a pretty quick study. In some areas."

"That must mean I need more lessons."

Her pulse jumped and quickened. Was he hinting at extending their agreement? Fatherhood lessons part two? She opened the oven and garlic-scented steam escaped into the room.

"I want to be the kind of parent who is involved with his kid's life and activities. I want Jax to be happy and have fun and get to try the things that interest him. Not only the things I want or think he should do."

"Those are very good goals. I'm sorry your parents didn't encourage all of your interests."

He shrugged. "The road behind me is paved with rules and a long list of dos and don'ts. Someone else's dreams and expectations. No one ever asked me who or what I wanted to be. It was just expected that I would follow happily along with my parents' wishes. In their footsteps."

"I'd say opening your gallery in Oak Hollow is a step toward following your own dreams."

He rubbed his chin and stared off into space and then made a sound as if he hadn't thought of that.

She gave the sauce one more stir, then sat in the chair across from him. "My mom was a school-teacher, so I guess I kind of followed in hers."

"But you don't love it?"

Now it was her turn to shrug. "I wouldn't use the word *love*."

"You told me your dress shop is your passion, and you seem to be happy there."

"I practically grew up there because I loved being with my grandmother and helping her at the shop. I'm so thankful that she left it to me."

He scratched his stubbled cheek and seemed to consider what she'd said. "I probably sound like I'm not thankful for the opportunities I've been given."

"But working at the auction house is not the thing you would have picked if you had a choice?"

"I never really felt like I had a choice." He grinned. "You should've seen them flip out when I told them about my interest in blacksmithing."

"Blacksmithing?"

"Yes. Metalwork. Forging."

"I know what it is. I just can't picture you doing it." *At least I shouldn't.* Because all she could envision was a shirtless Nicholas, toned muscles straining and shiny with sweat from the heat of the fire. Hammer strikes ringing out and his muscles straining with each hit.

"I saw a blacksmith shop in town, and I've thought about stopping by to see if they are looking for an apprentice, but that's off the table now. I need to focus on Jax and don't have time for extra hobbies."

"I can introduce you. Maybe you could at least observe or something while I watch the baby." She'd never been inside the blacksmith shop and didn't really know how it was done in modern times, but she was sure there were safety precautions like protective clothing and such, which would ruin her shirtless fantasy. And she preferred her vision of the glistening muscles of his bare back while he worked. "Your parents have very specific ideas of what you should and should not do or be."

"That's a true statement. My father inherited the family business from his father, who inherited it from his."

"So, a long line of Wellers have sat on the throne so to speak."

He chuckled. "I hadn't thought of it that way, but it's pretty accurate. I've always had to work to fit in with their world." With his hands flat on the table, he spread his fingers as if he was trying to figure out what he might use them for.

Another dangerous image popped into her head. His hands on her body, sliding along sensitive skin. She quickly shook off that thought. *Get a grip! That's a terrible idea.* "When you first came to Oak Hollow, you certainly gave the appearance of fitting into that world."

"Did I? I've never known any different. I guess we all deal with what we were given in life."

Deal with? She rubbed her forehead in an attempt to cover what was no doubt a bemused expression. He was talking as if his wealthy lifestyle was a challenge. When she once again looked at him, he was smiling at her.

"But I'm discovering a different world. One I like very much. Well…except for the lack of furniture and a TV," he said with a laugh. "Parenting doesn't leave much time or energy for shopping."

The oven timer rang. "Time to eat," she said quickly.

Before I think too much about keeping him in my world. And before she offered her guest room bed and anytime-use of her TV.

It was after midnight and Emma was exhausted but unable to sleep. She tossed aside her covers and went out into the backyard filled with night sounds and the soft scent of summer flowers on the warm breeze. And the sound of Jax crying. She settled into a lounge chair by the firepit that she'd helped Steven build a week after they'd moved in. The thought of him made her look at the row of trees along her back fence. One for each year she'd been without her family. Three red oaks alternating with three crepe myrtles with their pink blooms shimmering in the moonlight.

Later in the summer, it would be time to plant two more. Her tradition had started only a few days after she'd healed enough physically and when she'd needed something to keep her busy. Something to honor her husband and child. Emma couldn't explain to others why it gave her comfort, but it had become an important tradition she wouldn't miss for anything. Digging the holes was hard, sweaty work, but she liked to plant the trees all by herself. That way she could cry or talk to Steven and Rose or whatever struck her in the moment and not worry about what others thought. Someday the trees would wrap around her whole backyard, and she'd have to start in the front. Then maybe even ask neighbors if they wanted new trees in their yards.

The baby's crying went on for a while longer and was joined by Nicholas's voice attempting to comfort his son. They walked back and forth past the apartment window. First with Jax cradled against the center of his chest, then in the crook of his arm and then to his shoulder. Pressing her hands on the armrests in an effort to stand, she paused and stayed where she was.

I should let him work through this on his own. Like letting a baby cry it out.

But after three more minutes, she couldn't stand to hear any more of the baby's cries and the father's frustrated attempts to calm him. Blame it on a lack of sleep—and possibly really poor judgment—but she went up the stairs. She was supposed to be teaching him and the least she could do was give him a couple of pointers. After a few minutes of instruction, she would definitely go back to bed in her own house.

There would be no hanging around to talk to him. And no staying to flirt or be flirted with.

Chapter Seven

Nicholas started at the knock on his door but answered quickly, more than happy to see Emma's pretty makeup-free face. Her blue-and-white pajama shorts and tank top skimmed her curves and showed off a lot of her shapely legs. The pajamas were sexy without being an in-your-face invitation. Her pale hair was tumbling around her shoulders, waves curling over her breasts and drawing his eyes to places they should not be.

"My son hates me." He stepped back, hoping she'd come inside and share some wisdom. Plus, he didn't want to be alone.

"No, he does not hate you. He's just doing what

babies do." Emma closed the door behind her. "But Jax could be feeling some of your tension."

There was definitely tension in the air, but with her in the room, it was becoming a different kind of tension. Something that had been brewing between them since the first time she'd scowled at him across a table at his first small-business owners' meeting. This was a much more enjoyable tension that started in the center of his stomach and worked its way to all parts of his body. Some more so than others.

Dude, that is not why she is here.

But this new awareness in the air was something he could get used to. More tempting than the tastiest desserts.

"Can I try?" At his nod, Emma took the baby into her arms and kissed his forehead. "Hello, little sweetie. Let's see if we can figure out what you need." She sat on the couch beside Nicholas's rumpled pillow, put the baby on her shoulder and rubbed his back. "You didn't want to unfold the sofa bed?"

"Oh, I tried that," he said over his son's crying and rubbed his own back where the metal bar had tortured him. "But it's more comfortable with my feet sticking off the end than folded out." He plopped onto the other end of the couch. "A good mattress is at the top of my list of things to buy."

"Sorry. I should've told you about the unfortunate quality of the couch before you moved in."

The way she so innocently chewed the corner of

FREE BOOKS GIVEAWAY

2 FREE ROMANCE BOOKS!

2 FREE WHOLESOME ROMANCE BOOKS!

GET UP TO FOUR FREE BOOKS & TWO FREE GIFTS WORTH OVER $20!

We pay for everything!

See Details Inside

Complete the survey below and return it today to receive up to 4 FREE BOOKS and FREE GIFTS guaranteed!

FREE BOOKS GIVEAWAY
Reader Survey

1

Do you prefer stories with happy endings?

◯ YES   ◯ NO

2

Do you share your favorite books with friends?

◯ YES   ◯ NO

3

Do you often choose to read instead of watching TV?

◯ YES   ◯ NO

YES! Please send me my Free Rewards, consisting of **2 Free Books from each series I select** and **Free Mystery Gifts**. I understand that I am under no obligation to buy anything, no purchase necessary see terms and conditions for details.

❏ **Harlequin® Special Edition** (235/335 HDL GRQ6)
❏ **Harlequin® Heartwarming™ Larger-Print** (161/361 HDL GRQ6)
❏ **Try Both** (235/335 & 161/361 HDL GRRJ)

FIRST NAME	LAST NAME

ADDRESS

APT.#	CITY

STATE/PROV.	ZIP/POSTAL CODE

EMAIL ❏   Please check this box if you would like to receive newsletters and promotional emails from Harlequin Enterprises ULC and its affiliates. You can unsubscribe anytime.

SE/HW-122-FBG22

her lower lip was driving him crazy. "It's all fine. I practically followed you home like a puppy, and beggars can't be choosy. I'll get it all figured out."

"Tomorrow, we'll blow up the air mattress and bring it up here. It's not perfect but some better."

"If you insist," he said with a dramatic sigh.

She laughed. "You are impossible."

Jax stiffened against her and gave an extra-loud squawk.

"I don't know what to do for him," Nicholas said. "He wouldn't finish his bottle. And I changed his diaper, but he still isn't happy."

"Did you burp him?"

"I tried, but he didn't burp."

"Let's try a different hold." She sat his little bottom on her lap, palmed his torso with one hand and leaned him forward while patting his back with her other. The baby emitted a loud belch and a toot, one right after the other.

"Nice job, son. And you, too," he said to Emma.

"Well, thank you." Turning Jax around, she lifted him enough to kiss his forehead. "Your daddy wasn't doing so bad before I came up here, was he?" Jax yawned and stared at her with curious eyes as he grabbed a fistful of her long hair.

Apparently, his son was as fascinated by Emma as he was. He wouldn't mind getting his hands on her hair, either. Then he could see if it was as soft as it looked, and what her reaction would be if he twirled a curl around his finger and gave it a little tug. His blood heated.

She untangled Jax's tiny fingers from her hair, cradled him in her arms and rocked him slowly. "That's better, isn't it, sweetie?"

"He sure is cute when he's not crying." Being a single father was something he'd never, ever considered. He'd never thought to be a father at all, but now that it had happened, he sure did wish his child had a mother. A mother like Aurora would have been. Like Emma would be.

"He seems to like it when you sing to him," she said.

"You heard that?"

"I did." One corner of her mouth turned up. "I believe it was a Coldplay song."

"I don't know any lullabies, and it just popped into my head."

"It was good, and you have a nice voice. You can sing anything, except maybe heavy metal." She demonstrated by singing "At Last," the Etta James song her grandparents had loved to dance to. Jax eagerly started sucking on the bottle she offered, and she kept singing.

Her lovely voice sent a wave of warmth through him and loosened the anxiety banding his chest. There was a spark in the air, and he found himself leaning in her direction, hoping to catch more of her vanilla-and-peaches scent. He raised a hand to see if his son would grasp his finger, but with his tiny hands being so close to Emma's full breasts, Nicholas decided against it. There was too much risk of one of them getting the wrong idea. Mainly him. Because if she responded in any receptive manner at all, he would be hard-pressed not to see if she tasted as good as she smelled. Like baking and home and sexy woman all rolled into one delicious recipe.

"I'll probably never be able to thank you enough for helping me with my surprise fatherhood. It sounds cliché, but I don't know what I'd do without you." And he didn't want to find out.

"I'm glad it's summertime and I'm able to help. Everyone needs a little advice and a helping hand now and then. Maybe you can pay me back by giving me a hand when I need it with some other projects around here."

"I'd love to give you a hand." He could think of a whole list of things to do with his hands. All the ways he could touch her and see how she'd respond and what noises she'd make. He caught sight of the pretty, pink blush blooming on her cheeks before she refocused on the baby she was feeding. Was she having the same thoughts? Were her cheeks as warm as they looked? Nicholas wanted so badly to press his lips to her rosy skin and kiss his way down her graceful neck.

"I think he's feeling better and worn himself out with all the crying." Emma once again put him on her shoulder and patted his back. "You should both be able to get some sleep now."

Fat chance of that.

His body was way too revved up to fall asleep. "I know why I'm awake at one thirty in the morning, but what has you up at this hour? Could you hear Jax crying from your bedroom? Did he wake you, too?"

"No. I couldn't sleep and went out into the back-yard. That's when I heard him. And you."

"Are you a night owl?"

"No." Her brow creased. "Not normally."

What isn't she saying? "I hope it's not my intru-sion into your life that has kept you from sleeping."

Without answering, she slowly rose and eased the sleeping baby into his bed. "Sweet dreams until sun-beams find you."

He liked that saying. It was a nice way to say good-night to your child and he just might steal it. "I'm going to have a whiskey on the rocks. Can I get you one, too? Or something else to drink?" It was unfair, but he didn't want her to leave.

"I'll try what you're having, but a small shot for me, please."

He went into the small open-concept kitchen and pulled out the bottle, an ice tray and two glasses. "Sorry I don't have fancy glasses."

"I think I'll forgive you for that."

"Tomorrow I should be getting the results of the DNA test."

"Are you worried?"

"No. He's mine, but it will be good to get all the legal stuff worked out." He handed her the drink and took his seat on the other end of the couch. "Didn't you say you have a list of safe cars?"

Her smile grew wide as if his question pleased her. "I do. I'll give it to you tomorrow."

By the time she went back to her own house, he felt like he deserved an award for showing an amazing amount of self-control. He had successfully resisted his desire to make love to the woman who had captured his heart and mind.

The following day was once again an exercise in resisting his attraction for a woman he wanted—which was something he usually didn't have to do. He'd always let himself go for what he wanted in the romance area. And looking back, that lifestyle probably had a lot to do with his declining performance at work and his father's decision to make him take a look at himself. If he was being honest, he was learning a lot about the man he was and who he wanted to be, but he was nowhere near ready to thank his father for any of his actions. Not when he'd so coldly sent Aurora away. And although he tried not to be, he was angry at Aurora for taking the money and so easily cutting him from her life.

He rinsed a plate and put it into the dishwasher.

"Thanks for doing the dishes," Emma said and put leftovers in the refrigerator.

"No problem." Nicholas dunked the lasagna pan in the soapy water and took out some of his pent-up frustration by scrubbing the stuck-on cheese.

"I'll go check on the baby," she said and passed by so closely they almost touched.

Every time he had the urge to reach out and touch Emma, he pushed aside his own desires for her sake. And when his lips ached with the need to connect with hers, he thought hard about what he'd promised himself he'd do for Emma: give her time and not push her out of her comfort zone.

But maybe what she needed was to be pushed out of her comfort zone just like he had been?

That could be fun for both of us.

Nicholas winced. That was not the direction his thoughts should be going. He turned the pan around in the soapy water and attacked it from another angle. His time here was turning out to be good practice for how he wanted to live his life. An exercise in restraint and controlling every whim that struck him. Thinking about someone other than himself. Considering what Jax and Emma needed was giving him a new perspective about life. And in the future, he would make more of an effort to think beyond his own selfishness.

"I think that pan is clean enough," Emma said from behind him.

Slightly embarrassed that he'd been caught washing the same pan for five minutes, he rinsed it and set it on the drain rack.

"I need to walk over to my parents' house, check things and water their plants. Want to put Jax in the stroller and come along?"

"Sure." He closed the dishwasher—that she'd had to teach him how to load and start. "Your parents live within walking distance?"

"Yes. But they're away for the whole summer on a cross-country RV trip, and I'm looking after their house." She went into the living room, lifted Jax from his bassinet and gave him the sweetest smile.

With a sleeping baby in the stroller, they walked along her street in a comfortable silence. Light from the full moon sifted through the tree branches and made shapes and shadows dance across the ground. They caught bits of conversations or a TV playing now and then, and the air was scented with family dinners, freshly mown grass and summer flowers.

Walking beside this amazing woman and his sleeping child, he once again felt as if he were in a painting, and this time it was more Norman Rockwell or Currier & Ives. A brief sensation of weightlessness swept through him like a swift wind, and he felt…rich in a way he never had before. Lucky, not because he'd grown up in wealth and privilege, but because he was getting to spend time with Emma.

He didn't want it to end, and that was another good reason not to push her.

"Here we are," she said and went up the front walk of a red-brick Tudor.

"This is the house where you grew up?"

"Yes." Her key snicked in the lock. "I also spent a lot of time at my grandparents' house, which is now mine."

When the interior lights flipped on, he was hit with a welcoming, cozy feeling, like everything was ready to be used and enjoyed. Plush leather furniture, drink coasters on the coffee table and fluffy blankets draped over matching reading chairs that faced a well-used fireplace. A basket of knitting rested beside one chair and fishing magazines beside the other, and it gave the impression that Emma's parents enjoyed their downtime together. Not in separate rooms like his parents.

"Make yourself at home while I get everything done." Emma tossed him a green Jolly Rancher from a bowl by the door and popped a red one in her mouth on her way from the room.

He parked the stroller beside the couch and brushed a finger over his son's soft wisps of brown hair. "Sleep well, my little man."

The green apple candy was tart on his tongue and made him pucker. Nicholas took in the room as if there would be a test at the end of the night. The family photos scattered around the house were fun candid shots, not staged formal portraits like the ones at his parents' estate. Playing at the beach, Emma grinning without her two front teeth in front of a birthday cake and happy Christmases with smiling faces and torn wrapping paper scattered around. Emma walked through the room carrying a red watering can with a long, pointed spout, and when he caught her eye, they shared a brief smile.

Is she blushing again or just hot from the walk?

She returned a minute later with a folding three-step ladder and placed it under an ivy hanging high on a hook by the living room windows. The surroundings that were giving him a peek into Emma's life were suddenly forgotten, because all his focus was drawn to her climbing the stepladder. Her white shorts gave him a great view of very feminine legs.

While reaching to get the watering spout into the pot of ivy, she swayed, and water trickled down onto the stepladder.

He rushed forward. "Careful, Em. Let me help you with that before you fall."

She gasped as her flip-flop slipped, and he caught her, his arms banded under her nicely rounded butt, just as she dumped the water right over their heads.

"Oh my God," Emma squealed, and the watering can clattered against the wooden floor.

Her arms wrapped tightly around his head, pushing her breasts more firmly against his face, her scent of vanilla and peaches intensified by the water soaking into their shirts. Holding her body against his was a fiery shock to his system, and the cold water was the only thing keeping him from combusting. After a second of stunned silence, he let her curvy body slide slowly down his until her feet touched the floor, electricity arcing between them.

"I can't believe I drenched us," she said between giggles.

Laughter vibrated between them, and before he realized what was happening, her hands were tangled in his hair and her lips were on his, soft and sweet and tenderly potent. Blowing the lid off his self-control as desire rushed through him.

He cradled the back of her head, teasing her lips apart and losing himself in the flavor of her watermelon candy mixing with his green apple. Her soft moan like lightning danced between them. The eager sweep of her tongue across his. His sweet Em molded her curves against him, fitting perfectly, and potent desire pulsed through his veins.

The willpower he'd been working so hard to maintain disintegrated into vapor. Just when he was pulling her hips closer and deepening the kiss, her whole body went stiff, kind of like she'd done on the sidewalk at the square.

She stepped back from his embrace, a hand to her chest and breath ragged. "I'm so sorry. I'm acting like this plant is mistletoe. It's not even the right season for that." Emma shoved wet hair from her face, then crossed her arms as if she was cold. "Please, forget I did that."

The way his whole body had awakened, he would never forget that kiss, but that's not what she needed to hear right now. With a slow, deep inhale he forced himself to cool off. If he played it off as if nothing out of the ordinary had happened, hopefully it would ease her distress. She didn't have to know that their earth-shattering kiss had rocked his world.

"Forget what? That you dumped water on my head?" He rubbed a hand through his wet hair, flicking water into the air.

She exhaled slowly and attempted a smile, but it trembled around the edges. "I should get a towel."

He'd let himself get carried away, but her kiss had been bursting with passion he couldn't resist. The big question: Was her passion for *him*, or simply a long-overdue release of pent-up emotion?

Chapter Eight

Mortified was Emma's current state of being. Pressed against Nicholas, a mega blast of attraction had overtaken her senses. She'd lost her head and attacked the man with her mouth and hands. The evidence was in the way her lips pulsed, and she felt shimmery, like a glitter bomb had burst inside her. The heat of desire combined with embarrassment was mixing into a swirl of conflicting emotions.

What is wrong with me? So much for keeping him at a safe distance.

"Thanks for saving me from falling on my butt."

Nicholas smiled and cleared his throat before shoving his hands into the pockets of his cargo shorts. "Anytime. If you'll get a mop, I'll clean up the water while you finish the rest of your list."

She hurried away from him and stood in her parents' kitchen, tempted to dash out the back door or hide in the pantry and eat a box of cookies. There had been several times she'd been tempted to kiss him but always resisted. Being this close to him in a house she hadn't shared with Steven had been all it took to snap her control in a big way.

Way to embarrass yourself.

But Nicholas hadn't shoved her away. On the contrary. His passionate response had encouraged her further, and the memory of his talented mouth was enough to send sparks skittering across her skin. He'd gone out of his way to joke and lessen her embarrassment and was giving her what she needed in this moment. Respect. Time. Time to ease her way back into the world of romance and dating.

But is Nicholas Weller the right person to start with?

The next few days passed with their tentative friendship growing, and undertones of sexual tension were always shimmering in the air like pixie dust. They ate meals together, played with the baby and watched TV in the evening. They brushed against one another in the kitchen and when handing one another the baby, and every time was an exercise in self-control.

Neither of them mentioned the kiss, and somehow the baby lessons had extended beyond a week and developed to include cooking. Sharing meals had naturally evolved into cooking them together because, as she'd reminded him several times, she was not his personal chef. And while they chopped and measured and mixed, she enjoyed the sensation of having a crush on someone. The kind that made her check her appearance before joining him in the kitchen where the savory scent of bacon sizzled on the stovetop.

"I need a measuring cup for this waffle mix," Nicholas said.

They reached for the same drawer and their hands brushed. A high-watt sizzle vibrated between them, and she busied herself rummaging in the drawer, then placed two measuring cups beside the mixing bowl.

Focus, Emma. Find something to talk about that is not how much you want to relive that kiss. "Did you find any more pieces for the gallery?"

"Yes. I commissioned a painting from your friend Alexandra."

"That's wonderful. I love her work." She pulled the pan of bacon off the burner and put the pieces to drain on a paper-towel-lined plate. "Oh, that's the measuring cup for dry ingredients. Use the glass one for liquid measure."

He looked between the two cups. "That makes

sense." Once he'd filled the correct cup, he dumped milk into the bowl of powdered waffle mix. Some of it splashed out of the bowl, and he jumped back and checked the front of his pale green Prada T-shirt for stains.

Nicholas made her smile every day, and she rarely felt the urge to roll her eyes. "Would you like an apron? I have a lovely yellow one that belonged to my grandmother."

His eyes narrowed. "No. Thanks. This shirt happens to be machine washable." Grabbing the wooden spoon, he stirred the batter, the bits of blueberries turning the mixture a streaked lavender color.

He was right about being able to make a great sandwich, but that was where his talent in the kitchen ended. She pointed to her handy-dandy, no-mess batter dispenser. "Pour about half into that and hand it to me."

He did as she'd instructed, and as he passed the full gadget to her, he unknowingly squeezed the part of the handle that opened the valve on the bottom. Batter streamed from the opening, and she automatically reached out to catch the gooey mixture with her hands, but of course some of it ran through her fingers and onto the floor while most of the tiny blueberries stayed in the palms of her hands. Slightly stunned, she just stood there.

"Oh, shoot." He put the dispenser into the sink, and with a look of alarm, took several steps backward and chuckled. "Sorry. Maybe I do need an apron. I'm not dressed for this level of..." His mouth twitched and his eyes danced with a dare-you expression. "Messiness."

"Nick Weller, are you calling me a mess?" It sparked her playfulness, and this opportunity was simply too irresistible to pass up. With her sticky hands held out, she walked his way, not caring that more batter dripped onto the floor. "You look like you could use a hug."

"You wouldn't."

"You know, I think you're right," Emma said, and watched him relax, then immediately pressed her goo-covered hands against his T-shirt. His chest rose with a sudden inhale. "You're right that you aren't dressed for this messy activity."

He wrapped his arms around her, trapping her hands against him. "I can't believe you did that. You do know what they say about payback?"

She shivered and was tempted to ask what he had in mind. "Some say that it can be fun, and others say it's not very nice?" She slid her hands over his pecs to his shoulders, completely destroying his shirt with purple-blue streaks. But she'd seen the tear on the back that he didn't yet know about and knew he'd stop wearing it.

They were so close all she needed to do was raise onto her toes and her lips could meet his, but she'd been the one to attack him at her parents' house and wasn't going to be the aggressor again.

"Let's go with the it-can-be-fun version." He dipped his head and kissed her tenderly, softly sliding the tip of his tongue across her lower lip.

She shivered and poured her desire into the kiss, and her skin began to flame from the inside out. The level of talent this man possessed in his lips alone teased her with the promise of great pleasure.

The alarm on her phone chimed and made them both jump. "That's my get-ready-for-work alarm."

He quickly kissed her once more before letting go. "I'll pay you the rest of what I owe you later." He winked and pulled his dirty shirt over his head.

The sight of his bare torso made her seriously regret setting that stupid alarm.

They had done a good day's business, and Emma hadn't seen Nick and Jax since this morning when they'd made a mess of breakfast together, but that didn't mean she hadn't thought about them at least one hundred times since then. And by the time she got home from book club tonight, they'd be up in the apartment.

"I'm ready when you are," Jenny said from behind the register. "There is a glass of red wine calling my name."

"Same. Let's go." Emma flipped the sign to Closed and locked the door behind them, and they walked around the square toward Sip & Read. The evening air was warm and thick with the sweet aroma of homemade waffle cones drifting from the ice cream shop, but there was a yummy piece of cheesecake waiting for her at the bookstore's café.

"How do you think Nicholas will handle the evening all alone without your backup?" Jenny asked.

"He's done it before."

"But you're usually just steps away in the house or shop next door."

Emma chuckled. "True. I guess we shall see."

An older gentleman held the door of the bookstore and ushered them through ahead of him. "Thank you," they said to him in unison.

The other three book club members were already at their usual table in the romance section. Jessica, the town's veterinarian, was standing to unfold and show off the front and back of a green T-shirt advertising her clinic and wildlife rescue. Their musician and artist friend, Alexandra, had her long red hair pulled up into a messy bun secured with a paintbrush and a pencil poked through at odd angles. And because Tess was pregnant, she was sipping a sparkling mineral water instead of wine.

"Hello, lovely ladies," Jenny said as they drew close to the group. "I'm taking bets on whether Nicholas will call for help with the baby this evening, and if so, at what time."

Everyone laughed and started calling out times.

Emma smiled and chose eight thirty, but inside she couldn't deny hoping he would call and need her. Over their time together, she'd quickly stopped disliking him, then became charmed, and now she looked forward to seeing him. And missed him when she was away. Her stomach flipped at the same time her chest tightened.

Are we...dating? Is this the start of something?

"Emma," all her girlfriends said in singsong voices to get her attention.

"Sorry." A blush warmed her cheeks. "What did you ask me?"

"Tell us how it's going with your houseguest?" one of them asked.

"He's not my houseguest. He's renting the apartment above my garage."

"Then let's call him your sexy tenant?" Tess flashed her deep dimples. "When he came into the antique shop for a few pieces this morning, he was looking mighty tempting."

Emma could not deny that he often looked like a tasty Prada-covered snack.

"Sexy tenant. I like that nickname," Alexandra said and pulled the pencil from her hair and started sketching something on the back of a paper menu. "Is Nicholas as high maintenance as you thought he would be?"

Jessica laughed and tucked the green T-shirt into

her purse. "I can tell by the smile Emma is *attempting* to hide that this is going to be a good story."

Emma's insides swirled pleasantly. She was barely admitting her feelings to herself and was not ready to say it aloud to her friends. "He's not as bad as I first thought he'd be. A lot of what I first saw as cockiness is what was expected at his family's auction house. And I suspect it's also a layer of protection. He's more thoughtful than I would have guessed he'd be and has more skills than I anticipated."

"Oh my. Tell us more about these skills," Jenny requested, and they all leaned toward Emma like she was about to reveal a big secret.

Emma laughed. Their setting was way too public to discuss his superb kissing skills. "I'm talking about baby things. Diapering was a challenge at the start, but now he's got it down."

Thirty minutes later, Emma's phone rang, and their conversation paused. Nicholas's number appeared on the screen. "It's him."

Tess looked at her watch. "I win the bet."

"Hello," Emma said into the phone.

"Sorry to bother you during your girls' night, but I have one quick question."

Emma shushed her giggling friends. "What is it?"

"Where is the thermometer? The forehead one. *Not* the old-fashioned kind."

She would've laughed if she hadn't been worried. "Is he sick? What's happened?"

"I just want to check. He feels a little warm."

"It's in the medicine cabinet in the hallway bathroom."

"Is it okay if I go inside your house and get it?"

"Yes. You know where the spare key is hidden. I'll stay on the line while you check his temperature." She bit her fingernail, listening to Nick's feet clattering down the wooden staircase, Jax fussing and his daddy telling him everything would be okay. "How long has he been fussy?"

"Not long. He just woke up. He felt warmer than normal when I changed his diaper."

Her girlfriends quietly waited to hear what was happening, and she wished they'd go on with their conversation and stop watching her. Because all she wanted to do was grab her purse, throw down some money and rush home. She heard the thermometer beep.

"It's good," he said. "Normal temperature. You can go back to your regularly scheduled evening."

His statement made her smile, but she was still worried about Jax and fighting the urge to go home. When she ended the call, Emma glanced from friend to friend. "What?"

Jessica swirled wine around in her glass. "You really care about them, don't you?"

She sighed. "I guess I do."

"I'm sorry we've been teasing you," Alexandra

said and slid the paper menu sketch over to her. It was a cartoon version of Nicholas holding Jax.

Emma waved a hand. "It's fine. I know it's stupid to let myself get close to them."

"It is not stupid at all, and it's never wrong to care." Jenny leaned her shoulder against Emma's. "It's okay for you to let someone new into your life. Don't forget, I also knew Steven well enough to know he would want you to be happy. He would not want you to be lonely."

A tingle rippled across her skin and she touched the beads on her bracelet. "Steven always said, 'Try to find something good in every situation.' I guess I've forgotten that lately."

Their waitress arrived with a second bottle of wine and a tray loaded with savory snacks and decadent desserts. "Enjoy, ladies. Give me a shout if you need anything else."

"Thanks, we will," Emma said and practically dived into her slice of raspberry-covered cheesecake, the perfect mix of sweet and tart.

"If you like Nicholas and he is a good guy, I don't see anything wrong with allowing yourself to explore what might be between you," Tess said.

"I agree," said the other three women.

"It might turn out to be nothing more than flirting or friendship, but it could be fun. And even if he's not someone you end up with, he can help you get back out there."

Not knowing what to say, Emma took another bite of cheesecake. Her friends took the hint and started talking about the next book they wanted to read. It would be nice to have a romantic connection with someone again. To be treated like a woman and share intimate moments with a man. Maybe it was time.

But is Nick the right guy? Are my feelings for him real...or is part of it because he comes with Jax?

She pictured Nick playing with his son. Although she adored the baby, her feelings for the man were also real and separate from his child. Anxiety turned into excitement.

"Okay, ladies." Emma held up her glass. "Here's to letting myself be open to possibilities."

"Cheers."

Glasses clinked and Emma's next sip of wine tasted like hope and possibility.

Late that night, a loud bang startled Emma from a dream about rainbow-colored rabbits hopping out of a hollow log. Bolting upright, she jumped out of bed but stood there trying to orient herself.

"Emma, I need you. Em!"

Nick? The tone of his voice sent a cold lash of fear straight to her core. The panic in his voice had her rushing from her bedroom with her heart in her throat, and she almost ran into him at the end of the hallway. His eyes were wide as a full moon, and he clutched his crying and coughing infant to his bare chest.

"What's the matter? What happened?"

"He's coughing and it doesn't sound normal. What's wrong with him?"

She placed a hand on the baby's back and recognized the sound of a barking croup cough and forced herself to calm down enough to think. *Focus.* She said a quick, silent prayer that Jax would be okay. "I know what to do. Follow me." She led him into the master bathroom, slid back the shower door and turned the water to the hottest setting.

"Em, what are you doing? Shouldn't we be going to an emergency room or calling 911?"

With a whole lot more calm than she felt, she clasped Nick's face and made him look at her. "Take a breath. It will be okay. Step into the back of the shower where the water isn't hitting you."

Looking more than a little skeptical, he did as she asked.

After climbing in beside him, she closed the glass door. "His cough is caused by croup. It's much like the virus that causes the common cold. The steam will help with his breathing, and we'll go to the doctor first thing in the morning."

"Really? This will work?"

"If it doesn't help soon, I'll drive you. Turn Jax to face the steam." Nicholas shifted Jax, cradling the baby's back to his chest, supporting his bottom with one hand and the front of his torso with the other.

Jax's crying had stopped, but he made a squeaking sound on each in breath between coughs.

"That's it, sweetie. Breathe in the steam." She hummed to him and then softly sang the lullaby from the time she found him in the empty gallery. Within a few minutes, Jax wasn't coughing or squeaking.

The baby yawned, stretched his little arms and closed his big brown eyes.

"Let me hold him for a minute." Emma took the baby from Nick and nestled him in the crook of one arm, so thankful he was okay.

Nicholas tipped his head back against the tile wall and rubbed his sweaty face. He was wearing only a pair of running shorts and no shirt, so there was a lot of tanned skin on display. Trickles of sweat slid along the planes of his chest and into the waistband riding low on his hips—low enough to reveal the V-shaped muscle below his belly button.

A lovely feeling spiraled in her own belly. She jerked her wandering gaze to his face and was relieved to find his eyes still closed. Thankfully, she had not been caught checking him out. Nick was fiercely protective, thoughtful, funny and way sexier than was safe for her to be around. But also, if she wasn't mistaken, he was a little wounded and guarded. Like her. He was a 180-degree turnaround from the man she'd first thought he was.

Nicholas opened his eyes and reached out to cradle a hand around the top of his son's head. "He's okay?"

"Yes, but we should probably stay up to keep a close eye on him." Emma lifted her arm enough to kiss the baby's damp forehead. When she raised her head, Nicholas cupped her cheek, his thumb brushing the corner of her mouth and making her breath catch. If there wasn't a sick baby between them, she'd wrap herself around him like she'd done when she doused them with water. She would slide her hands up the length of his back, around his toned shoulders and down along his arms to link their fingers. Then she'd press her lips to his and lose herself in the warmth of his kiss.

His fingers trailed down the side of her neck, then still farther down her bare arm, liquid fire following the path of his touch, and as if he'd read her thoughts, he held her free hand.

"Em, I don't know what I'd do without you."

"I'm glad I could be here for you and Jax."

He brought their joined hands to his mouth and pressed a lingering kiss to her knuckles. "I'm so thankful you're the one who found Jax. I never would've thought to ask for your help otherwise, and…you are…our angel."

Lightness filled her chest, and she smiled. *Does he want to keep me in his life? In their lives?* They did live in the same small town, and both adored

Jax. Not to mention their businesses were side by side. As her girlfriends had just said at book club, they were both single adults, and she had just told them she would let herself be open to possibilities.

"You've been here from the start." With a quick squeeze to her hand, he let go and brushed damp hair from her cheek, letting his fingers linger on her skin. "From the first second of my unexpected fatherhood, you've been here for both of us."

Their connection certainly felt like a lot more than her services as a childcare teacher. "Right place, right time," she said and let her hand slide over the curve of his muscular shoulder.

"What if it's not just by chance?" he asked.

"What could it be? Fate? Destiny?" It could be the steamy heat or the late hour, but she was growing pleasantly dizzy.

"It could be." He leaned forward and pressed his lips to hers. Softly. So sweetly. "When I kiss you, it feels like something that is meant to happen."

She read the kiss as a question about her willingness to move things any further between them. She needed things clearly stated so she could be absolutely sure they were on the same page of their relationship story. "Nick, are you thanking me just for being your nanny?"

"Sweetheart, you've never been just a nanny. Look at you now." His eyes dipped to the baby cradled against her body. "Holding my baby so protectively while standing in a steamy shower in your pajamas because that's what he needs. You are an amazing woman."

His compliment quickened her heart rate. "You are pretty amazing, too. I'm really proud of how quickly you are learning how to take care of Jax. You probably won't need me much longer."

"Don't say that, because it's not true. It's not just Jax. I need you, Em. And more than that, I want you in my life."

Her breath stuttered. "You do?" The water had grown cold, and she momentarily considered handing him the baby so she could step back into the chilly spray and cool her fired-up libido.

When she shivered, he reached around her to turn off the water. "Yes, I do."

"I like having both of you in my life, too."

He grabbed a towel off a hook right outside of the shower, wrapped it around her shoulders and drew her into a loose hug with his son between them. "Can we stay down here with you for tonight?"

"Absolutely." She wouldn't have it any other way. "We can keep one another awake while we keep an eye on Jax. Just in case we need to get back in the shower." More shivers erupted across her body and this time it wasn't because she was cold. It was the image of just the two of them naked together in the shower. But now was not the time to live out that fantasy. It was time to take care of baby Jax.

They walked from the bathroom, and she started to lead him into her bedroom but changed directions and went into the guest room. She settled the sleeping baby in the middle of the king-size bed. "I'll get a fresh diaper and dry clothes."

"Before you go…" Nick slid his arms around her waist. "How about a hug?"

She eagerly encircled his neck and sighed when her body met his. "Would you like a kiss, too?"

His answer was a soft growl, and this time his kiss wasn't a soft brush of lips. It was filled with passion and fire and was heady with the promise of things to come, and they were both breathing heavily when they finally pulled apart.

"I should change my clothes now." Emma rushed from the room before she took things too far too fast.

With Jax sleeping peacefully in the center of the bed, they sat on either side of him, watching the rise and fall of his chest.

Still shirtless and tempting, Nicholas shifted to lie on his side and propped up on one forearm. "How did you know what to do tonight?"

"Baby books, fostering and taking care of my niece and nephew. My older brother's family used to live in Oak Hollow. Now they live in Nashville."

"My sister, Victoria, doesn't have any children. My parents have expressed their concern about neither of us having a child to carry on the Weller name."

"Then won't they be happy about Jax?"

"You would think so. And hopefully they will be eventually, but Jax arrived in an unacceptable way. In their minds, there should have been an engagement party, a big wedding, and then after the appropriate amount of time, a baby announcement. Everything in its proper order."

"I see. So, that's why you didn't want to ask them for help?"

"That and a few other things."

"You do know they are going to find out at some point."

"I'm hoping it's not until I know what the hell I'm doing."

She reached across the space between them and squeezed his hand, which rested below his son's tiny feet. "You're doing great and getting better every day."

Turning his hand in hers, he once again laced their fingers. "Without you, I would've had to run back home on the very first day." His smile managed to be both grateful and sexy. "I like being here with you."

Her nerve endings tingled. "I like it, too." They moved closer to one another until Jax was cocooned between their bodies, protected and safe. And loved.

"Tell me about your childhood growing up in Oak Hollow. Were you close to your brother?"

"Like your sister, he is a little over five years older than me. So, when I was little, he was my protector. But then I guess I became the pesky little sister who followed him and his friends around."

"I never really had that opportunity with my sister. Our activities and days were very scheduled and rarely included one another."

"Guess our childhoods were pretty different." The baby nuzzled against her in his sleep, and she kissed the top of his head. "Did you go to public school?"

"No. Private. For a while I even went to boarding school."

"Really?" She pulled up an image of him in a school uniform with a blazer and a tie, and she wanted to see a photo of him as a young boy. "Did you like it?"

"Not at all. Victoria liked it and was there years longer than I was."

When his foot slid across the bed to brush against hers, she was tempted to sigh. "Your parents let you come home?"

He chuckled softly and put a hand on his son's little round tummy. "Not by choice. I got kicked out."

Emma gasped but grinned. "For real? What did you do?" As a teacher she knew all about misbehaving children, and somehow it didn't surprise her that he'd been that kind of kid.

"Nothing too major. Just a bunch of small things that added up to my expulsion. The final straw was around Halloween when I put soap and red food coloring in the main water fountain in the center of the quad."

"Somehow, I can picture you doing that."

"My parents, as you can guess, were not at all happy, but my nanny was glad to have me home. She'd been doing other jobs around the house while I was gone. It was nice to have someone miss me. I still call her and visit her at her retirement home."

"I'm glad you have her in your life." She ached for the little boy who had just wanted someone to love and miss him. She hooked her lower leg across his.

"Did you like growing up in Oak Hollow?"

"As a child I loved it. It wasn't until I was a teenager that I wanted to see what was out there in the rest of the big, wide world. But I guess that's the case with most teenagers no matter where they grow up."

"And did you not like what you found? Is that why you returned home?"

"I enjoyed my time away at college and thought about staying in the city, but I came home after I graduated because my grandmother got sick. I took over the vintage shop, and then I got married and started my life here."

"Oak Hollow is a good place to start a life," he said, and with a sexy smile, he leaned across the baby and kissed her.

Her lips tingled with the promise of deeper kisses, and she returned his smile.

If he's starting a life here in Oak Hollow...

A flutter started in her chest. This could be the start of something new and wonderful.

Chapter Nine

Nicholas dozed off shortly before sunrise but when sunrays cut through the blinds, he woke to the sensation of his leg intertwined with someone else's and a baby's cooing. Before he could even open his eyes, he smiled. Contentment surrounded him like a cozy blanket. Blinking a few times to focus, he quickly forgot his lack of sleep. Jax was on the bed beside him eagerly trying to get all five toes into his mouth. Emma rested on her side facing them, her pretty face relaxed in sleep.

This is what my son deserves. To be encircled by two people who love him.

Every child and parent should have a chance to

make these kinds of moments and memories—minus the freak-out when croup appeared in the middle of the night. He hadn't known this kind of feeling existed, because if he had, he'd already be married with several children. He kissed his baby's chubby cheek and was glad there didn't seem to be any sign of fever.

He had little doubt that Emma loved Jax, too. She had technically known his son longer than he had.

She sighed, and when she opened her eyes and saw him looking at her, she smiled. "Good morning." Her hand went to Jax's tummy as if he was one of her first thoughts.

"Jax seems better," he said.

"That's often the case in the morning, but we still need to take him to see the doctor. We don't want another night like last night."

A cold shiver worked across his body. "It was the most scared I've been in my whole life." He let last night's fear and panic have one second of consideration before he pushed the memory away and turned his thoughts to better things. He rubbed his foot against hers. "But last night wasn't all bad. I enjoyed getting to know you better."

"Find something positive in every situation," she said. "That's what I'm going to try to do from now on."

Jax kicked his feet in tandem while making a noise that sounded like an owl hooting and they laughed. "He does that when I hold him up. It's like he's trying to hop instead of walk. He's like a little bunny." Nicholas sat up, held his son under his arms and put his feet on the bed. Jax didn't disappoint and immediately started trying to hop. "Are you my bunny boy?" he asked his son. When he glanced at Emma, she was frowning and touching the beads on her bracelet as she often did. "What's wrong?"

"Nothing."

"I can tell it's not nothing."

She pointed to the silver rabbit charm on her bracelet. "My husband's nickname for me was Bunny Rabbit."

"Em, I'm sorry. I won't call Jax that anymore."

She put a hand on his arm. "No. It's okay. Somehow, I think Steven would approve."

Jax began to fuss, and Nicholas got up to change his diaper. "Is that why you have rabbits all around the house and on your bracelet?"

"Yes. Most of them were gifts from him over the years." She climbed off the bed and stretched. "I'll go make his bottle and then call the doctor's office and leave a message."

He watched her leave the room and there was a lightness in his chest. At least she was talking about her husband and letting him into her thoughts and her life. This was progress, and even though he had a baby to take to the doctor, he felt good about where his life was headed.

* * *

Jax was cranky and had a runny nose but thank goodness there was no sign of the scary croup cough. They were standing outside of the white brick doctor's office when Dr. Roth-Hargrove parked her car. Her auburn hair was twisted into a low bun.

"She looks so familiar," he said to Emma.

"That's because she's Alexandra's mother."

"Now I see it. They sure do look alike."

She met them at the door with a comforting smile. "Good morning. Come inside and let's take a look at this little cutie and get him feeling better."

"Thank you so much for letting us get in for an appointment first thing," Emma said and introduced Nicholas and Jax.

They followed the doctor through the office to a Peter Rabbit–themed exam room they used for pediatric patients. "Have a seat in here and I'll be with you in a few minutes."

"Thanks," Nicholas said.

"More rabbits," she said under her breath. "I've never been in this exam room."

With his son in one arm, he pulled Emma in for a hug. "Do you think it's a sign or a coincidence?"

"I think it's a sign."

Savoring the feel of her lips against his, he sent thanks to heaven that this woman had come into their lives. There was a soft knock on the door, and they stepped apart.

Dr. Roth-Hargrove came into the exam room, her smile giving an air of comfort. "I see that your son had an appointment scheduled for later this week, but I guess he just couldn't wait to meet me. Tell me about his symptoms."

Emma explained what happened throughout the night as the doctor examined the baby.

"What you've described sounds exactly like croup."

"So, what we did last night was right?" Nicholas asked.

The doctor nodded. "You did everything right."

He looked at Emma and then took her hand. "I've been saying this a lot lately, but it's all thanks to this woman. I had no idea what to do."

"Sounds like you two guys are lucky to have found her."

"We sure are."

"I'm going to write a couple of prescriptions and give you a sheet of information and instructions. You'll need to sleep in the room with him tonight and keep the humidifier going."

His heart jumped behind his breastbone. "It might happen, again? The coughing?"

"It's possible, but now you know what to do. I can also recommend a great baby book for first-time parents."

"Probably a good idea," he said.

"I'll go gather everything you need," Dr. Roth-Hargrove said. "Meet me up front."

As she left the exam room, he put the diaper bag over his shoulder and Emma lifted Jax into her arms. When they stepped out of the exam room, the nurse practitioner, Gwen Clark, and her boyfriend, Christopher, were standing in the hallway and had just pulled back from a kiss.

Gwen was holding a bouquet of roses and looked surprised to see them. "Oh, I didn't know we had any patients yet."

Emma adjusted Jax in her arms. "We kind of snuck in ahead of our scheduled appointment."

The women walked together toward the front of the office, and the guys trailed behind them. "How's it going this morning?" he asked Christopher.

"Real good. I had to stop by and give my birthday girl some flowers before I head over to your gallery and finish the crown molding."

"Giving flowers to your girlfriend is important." *I should buy flowers for Emma.*

About the time they got back to Emma's house, the lack of sleep was hitting both of them. "Are you working today?" he asked while pouring himself another cup of coffee.

"I was going to go in and do inventory in the back, but I don't have to. There are two employees scheduled today. So, I think I'll call and tell them I need to stay home and to call if they need me."

Her yawn was contagious, and he copied her. "What I need to do can be done from here on my laptop and phone. Or it can all wait until tomorrow," he said and yawned again.

"Good. Let's both play hooky. Want to veg out in front of the TV for a movie marathon? Although we'll probably end up napping when Jax does."

The thought of spending the day tangled up with her on the sofa made him suddenly wide awake and rejuvenated. "Sounds perfect."

With snacks and drinks prepared, they put the bassinet beside the sofa.

"Would you and Jax like to stay down here again tonight?"

"Yes. Definitely." He'd just blurted that out without a second thought. *Way to sound desperate.*

"Good. Because I wasn't going to let you say no." She stretched out on the chaise lounge end of her sofa. "You can pick the first movie."

Would she laugh at his love of fantasy movies? "Let's watch *The Hobbit*."

"Good choice. I have the first and second movies on my DVR, but I haven't watched the second one yet."

"Oh, we need to fix that." *Score one for similar tastes in movies.* He lifted Jax from his blanket and, unsure how close to sit to Emma, he started for the center cushion, but when she grinned in a way that made his whole body hot, he chose the one closest to her. He held Jax up facing him, and his son blew raspberries and patted his tiny hands against Nicholas's face. "I'll cover your eyes for the scary parts," he said, then kissed the baby's cheeks until he giggled.

They stayed at Emma's that night, with him and Jax in the guest room and her in her own bedroom. The next night was the same—and filled with longing to be closer to her. And because he had only upgraded to a blow-up air mattress that needed to be reinflated every evening, staying in her house became their new normal. Their agreed-upon week of baby lessons had long since past, the garage was painted and Emma had not mentioned the end of their original deal. And he was not going to be the one to bring it up.

The summer afternoon was hot as usual, but a breeze blew and cooled his heated skin. Nicholas was carrying his son in the baby sling as they walked along the square. Emma put her arm through his and leaned in close enough to kiss Jax and then him. Her public display of affection made his heart flip-flop in his chest. This was a domestic scene he'd once wanted but had given up on long ago. And now, here was his chance to grab the dream he'd had as a young boy and saw others living in movies and storybooks.

Until his teenage self had started paying attention to his own family and had given up on that idea.

"I'm starving. What about you?" she asked as they entered her shop.

"I'm hungry, too. I'll go grab takeout from the Acorn Café."

"Great. I'll take a strawberry pecan salad, please."

"You got it."

He left her at the shop, and with Jax strapped to his chest, he headed across the center of the square to the Acorn Café. On his way out of the restaurant, Mrs. Jenkins—who he'd come to think of as leader of the small-town gossip committee—asked about Emma as if they were a couple. Did the whole town consider them an item? He liked that idea, because the thought of being without Emma made his stomach hurt.

It had started out with him needing her for baby lessons, but now, he didn't want to be without Emma whether she was helping him with Jax or not. And he didn't want anyone else's help. Only the golden-haired woman with the crystal-green eyes. Because if he was completely honest with himself, he wanted a lot more from Emma than temporary deals or lessons.

He spotted Alexandra's husband, Officer Luke Walker, pushing a baby stroller and walking with his son Cody. Nicholas glanced down at his own child softly snoring against his chest. The officer was in uniform, smiling and talking to his children, and he was the picture of what this small town had come to mean to Nicholas. It was easygoing, mostly friendly, quirky in the best ways and…

Happy.

He stopped midstep and almost stumbled. A rare feeling zapped the center of his chest.

Is this what real happiness is supposed to feel like?

He hadn't realized how discontented he'd been with his life. But now… He felt lighter. Freer. He wanted to smile more, laugh more.

Several people walked around him because he was still standing like a statue in the middle of the sidewalk. Nicholas glanced around to see if anyone else had noticed the sudden change in him. Did he look different? He felt different, and a weight had been lifted from his mind. This simple scene of an officer pushing a stroller around a square filled with historic buildings had him picturing a life here. Picturing his child's life here in Oak Hollow.

With Emma.

This little town that he'd once thought to get in and out of as quickly as possible had altered his way of thinking and ended up changing his life. His plan to build a successful business, prove himself and then go back and settle in to take over the Weller family auction house had been sidelined by a tiny infant, an amazing woman and the welcoming townsfolk of

Oak Hollow. In such a short time, he could no longer imagine returning to his old life and his old ways, working long hours and spending many evenings out at events. Chasing easy pleasure but not getting attached. An imitation of a happy life.

Someone walked past and said hello, calling him by name and pulling him from his thoughts and back into his surroundings. "Good afternoon," he said and waved to the man.

He didn't want late nights out on the town or party girls. He wanted nights spent putting his son to bed and then talking to Emma. Kissing her. Sleeping beside her like they'd done the night Jax got sick. Sleeping beside her skin to skin. The idea sent an electric jolt through him.

I don't need to be the CEO of a prestigious auction house to be content and happy. I need to build a life for my son where we'll both be happy.

But it was way too soon to say anything about this to Emma. So, out of caution, he'd keep his revelation to himself. He would not tell her that he envisioned the rest of his life in Oak Hollow with her.

I need to be patient until I know she's ready to move on and love again.

Emma carried a pair of black stiletto heels to the front display window and caught sight of Nick moving at a brisk pace along the sidewalk. He suddenly stopped and stared, but at what she couldn't tell.

What is he thinking about so hard? After a few moments, his stunned expression cleared, and he smiled big enough to make his eyes crinkle.

What just happened? Did I just witness some kind of epiphany moment? And where do I fit in?

Since she was still having doubts that she was ready for a serious relationship, something about this scene made her nervous. Like it or not, planned or not, she'd fallen for a motherless child and his handsome father. They were rapidly moving beyond friends who flirted and kissed, but if they had a real romantic relationship and then broke up, she'd lose another man and child in one swoop that could break her.

Taking a deep breath to calm her fluttering pulse, she opened the door for him. "That was fast service."

"Hope I earned a big tip." He winked and she chuckled. "Ready to eat?"

"Yes, definitely." She'd swear there was something new in his eyes and his step. A shift she couldn't put a finger on, but it made her blood tingle through her veins. "There are no customers at the moment, so let's eat while mine is still cold and yours is still hot."

"How do you know I didn't get a salad, too?"

She grinned. "Did you?"

"No, but it could happen."

She followed him back to the kitchenette. "What has you so happy all of a sudden, Mr. Weller?"

Without a word, he put the take-out bag on the table, kissed the top of his sleeping son's head and then kissed her with a soft brush of lips. "Life. And you."

Lovely tingles danced through her body. "Me?" She wanted to pull him in for a deeper kiss and see if she could discover the reason for the shift in his aura, but that would have to wait until they were alone.

"Yes. You and my little man." He unfolded the stroller that was propped in the corner and put Jax in it.

At the little bistro table, she pulled out her salad and his order of the chicken and dumplings daily special. "I like seeing you smile more than you used to. When you first arrived, you had sort of a…public expression. Like a mask to hide your true thoughts and feelings."

He grabbed drinks from the refrigerator and sat across from her. "My parents taught me to keep my emotions inside, and to put on, as you called it, a public face. But I don't want that for Jax."

Maybe his epiphany was only about becoming a father. "For the record, I like your real smile so much better."

"It feels better, too."

At closing time, Emma flipped the sign on the door. "Susan, will you get started on the closing list while I make a bottle and take it next door?"

"Of course. Take your time. And I'll be here for the opening shift tomorrow."

"Perfect. Saturdays can get busy." It was so nice to have a really good employee. Emma went into the back and started making a bottle. As much as she had originally hated that Nicholas outbid her for the retail space next door, having shops side by side had become very convenient for baby lessons. And having lunch together. And just popping in to say hello. Honestly, it was turning out to be an easy excuse for seeing Nick and Jax whenever she wanted, as if having them at her house wasn't enough.

I was supposed to be easing back into dating, but it appears that I've jumped in with both feet. And I don't know how to stop it.

With a warm bottle in hand, Emma went next door to the gallery, but stopped before going inside and watched Nicholas and Jax through the front plate-glass window. The baby was awake and in the Pack 'N Play that Nick had moved from the back office. He was kneeling and talking to his son with a smile on his face. He had become a wonderful father in such a short time. Better than she'd ever guessed he could be. He was also a good businessman and was creating a special place for people to gather, shop and appreciate wine and art. She needed to tell him she was proud of him, because she had a suspicion he didn't hear that enough.

On most days, they took turns carrying the baby

in the sling or letting him sleep in his Pack 'N Play in the back, and when one of them had something they needed to do, the other would watch him. And, of course, this had everyone in town talking. Old Mr. Williams had even asked her if she was the mother, like she and her flat stomach hadn't been in town this whole time. She shook her head at the memory and went inside the gallery.

"Who is ready for a bottle?" she asked. Jax cooed, and Nicholas flashed a quick sexy grin that made her lick her lips.

"Depends on which kind of bottle you're talking about," he said and lifted Jax into his arms. "I wish I was already stocked with wine."

"What has you so ready for a drink?" She moved close enough to hand him the bottle but instead of taking it, Nicholas used his free hand to sweep her hair back from her cheek. The brush of his fingers sliding across her jaw and trailing along the side of her neck sent a flutter of sensations to every part of her body, and she swayed forward.

Jax grabbed her shirt and babbled as if to tell her he wanted attention too.

"Hello, sweet boy. I'm glad to see you." She put the nipple in his mouth, and he eagerly started sucking.

Nick settled his son in the crook of one arm. "Although sharing wine with you sounds perfect, I want a few bottles to see how they look on the new wine rack."

Prying her attention away from the man currently stealing all her brain cells, she turned to the far-right side of the space where the bar and wine-tasting area was set up. "Oh, Eric finished it. It's gorgeous."

Made of a deep rich wood with art deco lines, the built-in wine rack was a showstopper. Most of the wine bottle slots were vertical but a scattering of horizontal spaces allowed for displaying the labels of featured wines and formed the shape of the winery's logo.

"It turned out great, didn't it?" His smile was proud, and he put an arm around her shoulders.

"Absolutely." Enjoying the warmth of his body, she leaned into him.

"Everything is on track to be finished in plenty of time for the opening."

"Did you invite your family?" She felt his body tense up and wished she'd kept quiet. She knew his family was a touchy subject and hadn't meant to bring down his good mood.

"Not yet."

"What if they find out about it?"

"Oak Hollow news is unlikely to make it to my parents."

She wouldn't say anything more about his family or who was invited. "I'll admit that I had my doubts about this place when you bought it."

"Really? Why?"

"Because I was a touch jealous that you were able to offer more than me. This place is going to be a big hit."

"Wait, let's back up to the 'offered more than me' part." He held her gaze. "You wanted this space?"

"Well…yes. We were going to expand, but—"

"Em, I'm so sorry. I didn't know."

His apology was genuine, and it made her smile. "Everything has worked out as it should. No apology necessary." She kissed the center of Jax's forehead as he drank his bottle. "I need about twenty more minutes in my shop before I can leave. I can meet you at home if you want to get a head start."

"We'll wait for you."

But will you wait for me to be ready for love again? She rushed from the gallery before her expression could give away her thoughts.

Just after her employee left, Nicholas pushed the stroller through the doorway of her shop then walked up behind Emma at the register and wrapped his arms around her waist. "Are you busy on Saturday night?"

"I don't have any plans." With her head tipped back on his shoulder, she inhaled his scent and told herself not to get her hopes up that it was anything special for her. "Do you need me to babysit?"

"No. My friend out at Deco Vineyard called and

invited me to a wedding. There will be a few people there he wants me to meet. Apparently, they're art dealers and wine lovers and perfect to have as customers or investors. And I'd like for you to go with me."

"Like a…" *Date?* She turned in his arms and bit her lower lip.

"Like a date," he said and grinned. "I just got off the phone with Eric, and he's offered to babysit so we can go without risking a crying baby at a wedding ceremony."

If he'd arranged babysitting, he must really want her to go. Otherwise, he would've asked her to watch Jax. "I'd love to go. When did you say it is?"

"Tomorrow night."

They walked home, cooked together, watched an episode of *Virgin River* and then went to their own bedrooms. Every night it was getting harder and harder to separate after a kiss at their doorways, and every night she thought about joining him in his bed, but a fear of messing things up and getting hurt always held her back.

When Emma couldn't sleep, she opened her closet and stared at her choices for an outdoor, evening wedding. She finally decided on her pale blue dress with the cherry blossom branches sweeping across the fabric. It lifted her breasts without being too revealing, hugged her torso, then flowed into a full skirt to midcalf. Since the wedding was outdoors, and no one liked to have the heel of their best shoes sink in the dirt, she chose her silver wedge sandals.

The last time she'd had a "first date" was in high school. And it had been with the man she married. *Is that why I'm so nervous?*

On the wall beside her closet door was an eight-by-ten photograph of a wild rabbit. She traced her finger across the glass, remembering when Steven gave it to her. He'd taken it himself while he was out on the job. "I'm seeing rabbits everywhere lately. I wish I could know for sure what it means. Are you trying to tell me something?"

Chapter Ten

Late Saturday afternoon, Nicholas packed a diaper bag and took Jax over to Eric and Jenny's house. Their four-year-old daughter, Lilly, was thrilled about having the baby at her house and promised to read him fifty books. He smiled at the memory. With a bouquet of colorful summer flowers in hand and his nerves kicking up like he was a teenager about to speak to a stern father before picking up his prom date, he adjusted the sky blue tie he'd picked out in the hopes Emma would like it.

"Should I ring the front doorbell or just go inside like I usually do?"

Since no one was around to give advice, he went

in through the kitchen and waited in the living room. When Emma came in, he was tempted to whistle. "Wow. You are so beautiful."

"Thank you."

Her blush was almost the same shade as the cherry blossoms on her pale blue dress. He gave himself a pat on the back for picking a tie that matched her outfit. In a pair of wedge heels, she stood at the perfect height to tip up her head and kiss him. Her blond hair was loose, just the way he liked it, and she'd even painted her fingernails. She was glamorous and would have fit in at any of the fancy events he used to frequent.

He held out the flowers and loved the way she smiled. "These aren't as pretty as you, but they smell nice."

She brought the bouquet to her nose. "They're beautiful and they do smell divine. I should put them in a vase before we go." She went into the kitchen and opened a cabinet. "Can you reach that crystal vase on the top shelf? If not, I can get the stepladder."

"I'll get it, and you should consider not using stepladders if I'm not around to catch you." The moment the words cleared his mouth, he wished to recall them. "I'm just kidding, by the way. I'm not trying to tell you what to do."

She stifled a laugh. "I'm not easily offended when I know how the comment was intended. You have witnessed a couple of incidents where ladders and I are not a good match."

She probably had no idea what a refreshing change her attitude was. Too many of the women he'd dated would've taken offense. He put the vase in the sink and turned on the water while she cut the ends of the stems and then arranged them.

"I didn't think I would feel so anxious about leaving Jax with someone," he said. "Even when I know they will take good care of him."

"It's natural." She washed and dried her hands, then smoothed them across the lapels of his charcoal gray suit coat. "Nice tie. You know… At first, I wasn't a fan of you wearing a suit around Oak Hollow, but now I see that I was wrong. You look very handsome."

He raised one eyebrow. "Why didn't you like my suits?"

"It's not that I didn't like the suits. They are beautiful. You were just overdressed for our town." With one quick kiss on his lips, she spun away and grabbed a small sparkly purse.

When he opened the passenger door of his Corvette, Emma hesitated. "Do you not want to go in my car?" They always took hers, but he loved his car and wanted her to like it too.

"Oh, no. Yours is fine." She gathered her skirt and eased down onto the low seat.

With the radio playing a country song, he backed down her long driveway and they were on their way.

"This is a cool car. I can see why you love it. You really restored it all yourself?"

"Yes, I did. It took a long time." He watched her delicate hand brush over the dashboard.

"Eyes on the road, not me," she said with a touch of fear in her tone.

"Yes, ma'am." She certainly was a nervous passenger. "It's hard to keep my eyes off you when you look so gorgeous."

"Well, you are going to have to. Safety first."

At the last stoplight on the way out of town, their light turned green, but when another car ran their red light, he hit the brakes hard.

"Nooo!" Emma screamed and covered her face.

Her reaction startled him so badly that he pulled into the parking lot of a grocery store and took a deep breath to unwedge his heart from his throat. "Em, I'm so sorry. I didn't mean to scare you."

Trembling and pale as milk, she put both hands on his cheeks. "You're okay?"

She is worried about me? "Yes, I'm fine, honey." He wrapped his arms around her and held her as much as he could across the center console. "And you are safe, too."

After a minute, her breathing slowed, and she sat back in her seat. "Sorry. I was in a bad accident and sometimes I just get freaked out. I'm fine now."

Suddenly, he remembered Eric saying her husband had died in a car accident. Had she been in the car with him? "We can go home if you want to."

"No. We need a night out. Let's keep going."

He pulled out onto the road and drove with extra caution.

"Nick, you can't drive Jax around in this car. It's just not safe for a baby in a car seat."

"I know. I've been looking at that list you gave me and know what I want to get. It's an SUV similar to yours." She was right. Their safety came first. Plus, three people couldn't fit in this car. But he sure didn't want to sell his Corvette. He would store this car in the garage at his parents' house and buy a second one.

Deco Vineyard was a sprawling place in the heart of the Hill Country. Rows of grapes curved over the land and into the sunset sinking behind the hills. The main building was a huge timber-and-stone structure built to look as if it had been there for a hundred years or more. A flower-covered arbor was set before rows of white chairs, and floral arrangements in jewel tones were scattered throughout the venue. The ceremony was short but beautiful, the food was delicious, and he had the prettiest date at the whole place.

While Emma was talking to a group of women who wanted to make plans for a day at her dress shop, Nicholas made his way to the outdoor bar for a scotch.

The bride's grandfather, an elderly gentleman in a black tux and walking with a silver-tipped cane, came up to the bar for his own drink. "It's nice to see so much love in the air. I'm Samuel DeWitt."

"Nice to meet you. I'm Nicholas Weller," he said, and they shook hands.

"You and your wife are a lovely couple. Do you have any children?"

Never before had he been happy about someone being mistaken for his wife, but this time he felt his chest puff up with pride. "She is most definitely lovely inside and out, but we aren't married."

"Well, young man, you better get on that before she gets away. Yours aren't the only eyes following her around tonight."

His first reaction was a flash of jealousy, and he had the urge to ask who was staring at her, but he quickly realized it was impossible not to notice the beautiful aura she projected, and he was proud to be seen with her.

How am I even thinking about marriage so quickly after meeting her?

"We haven't known each other for very long," he said to Mr. DeWitt.

The man laughed and motioned for Nicholas to follow him to the nearest empty table. "Only takes the blink of an eye to fall in love. I've been married to my girlfriend for almost sixty years." He pointed to a petite woman with silver hair swirled into a fancy updo.

The adoration in the older man's eyes was almost tangible. *Is this what a lifetime of love looks like?* "And you still call her your girlfriend?"

"Keeps things fun." His chuckle was gravelly, and he took a sip of his drink. "I can see the love in the way you look at your young lady. You don't want to stay a lonely bachelor forever."

Lonely? Has this man lived enough life to recognize what I've been hiding from myself until recently?

"And you don't want to wait too long and not have kids. Watching my granddaughter get married has been a wonderful day."

The unsolicited advice—that he'd normally roll his eyes at—was making him think harder about his and his son's futures. "Are you good at keeping secrets?"

"Son, I'm eighty. I have enough secrets to write a whole series of books." His golden wedding band clinked against his glass of whiskey as if making a point. "Tell me."

"I have a baby boy. I didn't even know he existed until recently."

"I take it this young lady is not the mother?"

"No."

"Is the baby the secret?"

He shook his head. "No. Emma has been teaching me how to take care of him. He's with one of our friends for the evening."

"Where is his mother?"

"That's where the secret comes in. But *scandal* might be a better word than *secret*."

Mr. DeWitt leaned in like he was ready for a juicy story. "Haven't heard one of those in a while."

"This one might be a good one for your novel, but people will think it's fiction. And it's sad. I was dating a woman who suddenly broke up with me and it didn't add up. Turns out, my father paid her to go away. Then she discovered she was pregnant and then in a terrible twist of fate, she died."

"Oh, no. I'm real sorry to hear about his mother."

"Thanks."

"But you know, young man, fate does have a way of twisting things in the right direction. Don't ignore the signs."

Could Emma finding Jax be fate working its magic?

Once Emma finished her conversation and came to find him, Nicholas held out his hand. "Dance with me?" All he wanted to do was hold her tight and consider Mr. DeWitt's advice.

"I'd like that."

They moved onto the dance floor under the starry sky. The red wine had deepened the color of her full lips to crimson, and he couldn't resist pulling her in a little closer to brush his mouth against hers. "Is it okay to kiss you in public?"

"Yes. It's more than okay." She tipped her head for one more kiss that wasn't as chaste as the first one. "Thank you for bringing me tonight. It's fun to get dressed up and go out with a handsome man."

"Happy to oblige. Anytime, sweetheart." With her head on his shoulder, he enjoyed the rest of their evening out.

It had become their routine to share a kiss in the hallway outside their bedrooms each night. Sometimes the kisses were harder to end than others. Tonight, Nicholas already knew how difficult it was going to be to sleep down the hall from her. So close, but just out of reach.

Emma had awakened on Sunday morning with a smile on her face and an extra shot of energy. After breakfast, she pulled the water hose across the backyard and around the firepit to the row of trees along her fence. Water splashed and soaked into the dirt around the tree she'd planted for her baby girl this time last year. She had been thinking a lot about her plan for Rose's unused nursery. It was time to do something about the closed door. Time to open it as well as herself to new possibilities. Especially now that Jax was getting too big for the bassinet, and there was a beautiful baby bed that wasn't being used.

Nicholas came out of the kitchen door with Jax

and spread a blanket for him on the grass in the shade. "Philip Deco asked me to come out to the winery again tomorrow. We need to spend the day going over some of the final details about the wine-tasting area of the gallery and our partnership. He also wants to meet Jax. Will you come with us?"

Their being gone for the day is a perfect chance to start my nursery project.

"Thanks for the offer, and I'd love to go back out there soon, but I have a special project I want to work on tomorrow." If she started on it while they weren't around, she wouldn't have to explain anything to Nicholas if she couldn't go through with it.

"Oh, yeah? What's your project?" He unkinked the water hose for her.

"I'd rather show you when it's done, if that's okay?"

"Of course. And you definitely deserve a day without us constantly in your way and underfoot."

"You two are saving me from summer boredom."

Something rustled in the leaves under a bush and they both turned to look as a small brown rabbit hopped out and stopped a little way from Jax's blanket as if he was inspecting the baby.

Emma's skin tingled and her heart raced. She always noticed anything to do with rabbits, but lately, they were everywhere.

The animal changed directions and hopped closer

to her and then behind the row of trees she was watering.

"Another rabbit," Nicholas said and smiled at her. "I think this one likes you."

"Maybe so."

"You should take it as a good sign."

"I think I will." She felt happy, and a sense of peace washed over her. She moved to water the next tree and turned to smile at him. Along the bottom of the kitchen door, some kind of white foam shimmered in the sunlight. "What in the world is that by the door?"

Nicholas turned to look and cursed before rushing for the house. When he opened the door, a glob of foamy white bubbles oozed over the threshold.

She turned off the water and picked up the baby. "What did your daddy do?" Jax grabbed her face and tried to gum her chin. "Since I left him doing breakfast dishes, I have a pretty good idea."

Nick appeared in the open doorway, and she couldn't help laughing as he used her broom to sweep more bubbles outside. Thankfully, it was mostly foam and not much water on the floor.

"You put liquid dish soap in the dishwasher, didn't you?"

"What makes you think that?" He gave her a lopsided grin. "I bet you're wishing for some of that boredom about now."

"I can see I still have more to teach you," she said with a laugh and kissed the baby's chubby cheek.

"For sure." More soap bubbles drifted into the breeze. "I think it might take months instead of weeks." He winked in a teasing way she'd grown to love.

It could take years. Or maybe forever. Is that too much to hope for?

Moving on did not mean losing any of her memories. She wasn't replacing her family. For the first time, she was finding the courage to start a new one.

The next morning Emma clicked Jax's car seat into the back of her SUV. "Be a good boy for your daddy." Nicholas was right behind her, and she stepped back to lean against him, and his arms slid around her waist. "You two have fun at the winery."

"Hopefully we'll get all our final plans hammered out."

"What time will you be home?" Her breath snagged as the word *home* echoed in her head, as if they were already a family, but he didn't seem to notice her moment of alarm.

"Late afternoon. I'll give you a call." With one soft kiss on her lips, he went around to the driver's seat, got in and backed down the driveway.

His bright red classic Corvette sat on the other side of the parking area. Shiny and flashy, just like Nicholas Weller had been when he arrived in town, but the man underneath all the flash was a good guy. One who, thankfully, had not said one word in opposition to her suggestion to borrow her car.

He also hadn't asked too many prying questions about her freak-out in his car on their way to the wedding. For a second, she'd considered telling him about the accident, but in the end, she hadn't been able to call up the words to describe the most horrific day of her life.

Pain burned in the back of her throat, and she touched each bead on her bracelet. The sound of a truck drew her attention and she waved Alexandra forward into the spot where her car had been.

"Sorry I'm a few minutes late," Alexandra said and closed the truck door behind her.

"You are right on time. How are the kids?"

"Good. Cody is fishing with his grandpa, and the baby is having some quality time with her daddy. I had to pump extra breast milk for Beth and that's what held me up."

"I know it's hard to get away when you have a new baby. Thanks so much for coming over to help me today."

"Of course. When you told me what you wanted to do, I was so excited to come and help."

"And I can't thank you enough."

When she'd told her friend the basics of her idea for the nursery, Alexandra had assured her she would bring everything they needed, and she hadn't been kidding. The bed of her husband's truck contained a large selection of paint cans, each with a different-colored swipe of pastel paint on the lid. There was also a plastic tub of brushes, rollers and a stack of canvas tarps.

"Show me the room we'll be working on, and then we can bring in all of the supplies."

She led Alexandra down the hallway and took a deep breath before opening the door. The flip of a switch illuminated the pink room that was stuck in time.

"Oh, Emma, this is beautiful. I can tell you worked hard on every detail."

"I did." And now, out of the beautiful room that existed, she wanted to create something new and magical. Something to help her move forward while still honoring her baby but also making it usable for another child. "But now it's just sitting here like a museum, and that's not helping anyone. Especially me moving forward with my life."

"Do you have any photographs of this room?" Alexandra asked.

"A few. Somewhere." Panic started to rise in her chest, and she swiped a tear. "Should I be doing this?"

"Hey, don't freak out. We're not going to change it so much that it's not recognizable. We're adding to it. Enhancing what you've already done."

"You're right." Emma straightened her spine and braced her hands on her hips. "Let's do this."

"Tell me more about what you envision."

"I'm hoping you can help me use the pink of this wall to create a pastel sunrise." She stepped forward and brushed her hand over the wall above the baby bed.

"That is a lovely idea." Alexandra wrapped one arm around Emma's shoulders for a side hug. "What gave you this idea?"

"A book I was reading to Jax." Even though he was too young to understand the story or words, she enjoyed reading to him. It was a special time to snuggle sweet baby Jax, and just thinking about it made her want to feel the weight of him in her arms. "It's time for a new beginning."

"A new day dawning," her friend said.

Warm tingles swept across Emma's whole body, and love shimmered like stardust. It was a dangerous thing to allow herself to get this close. To let a child who wasn't hers into her heart. But it had happened. "A new day dawning. I love that expression. Can we write it on the wall?"

"Of course." Alexandra turned to an adjoining wall. "What do you think about painting this one a pale green or yellow or blue, and then we can write the words there?"

"I think I'd like to paint it blue so it's like the

words are written in the sky. Maybe even with a few clouds."

"Perfect. What about the other two walls? Are we leaving them pink?"

Emma turned in a slow circle, taking in the details. The memories. The joy that had turned to unbearable pain. The numbness recently transformed into hope. Wounds, tears and heartbreak transforming her into who she was today. She paused on the photo of herself cradling her rounded belly and felt the sharp grab of the talons that accompanied her grief. The portrait was bittersweet. A reminder that she had carried and loved a child, even if only for a whisper of time.

She considered the idea of painting the other walls for several minutes before answering. With a deep sigh, she decided not to push herself too much all at once. "For today, I think I'll leave those two walls pink."

"Good decision. It's going to be beautiful. And remember, we can always do more later. Let's move the furniture to the other side of the room. I brought several large drop cloths, and we can cover everything."

They moved the baby bed, rocking chair and a few other pieces to the opposite side of the room and spread drop cloths on the wooden floor and furniture. Paint cans were lined up and brushes were ready.

"This is a special kind of VOC free paint, and the

odor will fade quickly and be safe by tomorrow, especially if after we're done, we open the windows and turn on the ceiling fan." Alexandra started opening cans with a small metal prying tool. "How are things going with Nicholas?"

Pulling her hair into a ponytail and giving herself a minute to think before speaking, Emma smiled. "He has been a most unexpected surprise. At first, I thought having him around was a nightmare, but now…" She sighed and her friend chuckled.

"And has the nightmare turned into a pleasant dream?"

"You know, I think it has." *A new day dawning. A new beginning.*

While Alexandra worked her artistic magic on the sunrise, Emma painted the adjoining wall a pale sky blue. With every stroke of the brush, she allowed her memories to come through. When she wanted to smile, she did. When she wanted to cry, she did. And when she came across a memory she wanted to share, she had a good friend willing to listen.

"Tell me more about Nicholas."

"That is somewhat complicated. But he is a good kisser."

Alexandra gasped and paint dripped from her brush onto the canvas tarp. "There's been kissing?"

"Have I not mentioned that yet?"

"Girl, you know you haven't." They both laughed. "But I had a feeling."

Nicholas had become so much more than the stranger she was teaching to take care of an infant. He was so much more than the shallow guy she'd once accused him of being. And as much as she'd tried to resist, Nick and Jax had stolen her heart. There had been no talk about Nicholas finding a place of his own. He wasn't even using the garage apartment anymore, but they were still sleeping in separate bedrooms. A bit of caution was still a must.

By the time Nick called to say they were on the way home, Alexandra had packed up and gone. He offered to pick up dinner and she eagerly accepted his suggestion. She left the ceiling fan running, closed the door to the nursery and hopped in the shower. When they arrived home, she was clean and dressed in yoga pants and a tank top.

Nick pulled dirty baby bottles out of the diaper bag and put them in the kitchen sink. "How did you do on your project?"

"Good. It went really well."

"Can I see?"

"Tomorrow. It's not one hundred percent done."

He pulled her in for a hug. "You should know I'm not the most patient man."

"Well, since I've taken on the monumental job of teaching you how to be a father, I must be honest and tell you that fatherhood requires a lot of patience. And actually, I don't think you give yourself enough credit. You have more patience than a lot of people I know."

Including herself, because with her sleeping down the hall from him, her patience was at a breaking point.

The next day, Jenny and one of their new employees were handling things at the dress shop while Emma stayed home to finish her project. Jax was home with her while Nick took a meeting at the gallery and received deliveries. The paint was dry, and Emma had swept, mopped, dusted and washed all the linens in the nursery. The furniture was back in place with the addition of new blue Peter Rabbit bedding.

The baby was having a late afternoon nap in the living room, and she was reading a book when Nick came in the back door. "Want to see my project, now?" she asked.

"Of course. But first I need kisses from both of you." He bent to kiss his sleeping child, then drew Emma into his embrace.

She sighed when his mouth met hers. Then, taking her hand, Nicholas followed her into the nursery and stood behind her with his arms wrapped around her waist. "Wow, honey. It looks amazing."

"Thank you. Since Jax is getting too big for his bassinet, I thought he could sleep in here tonight."

He turned her in his arms so he could see her face. "Are you sure?"

She kissed him softly and rested her head on his chest. "Read the saying on the wall."

"A new day dawning." He smiled down at her but when her lips trembled, he cupped her cheeks. "Hey, honey. Don't push yourself. If it's too soon—"

She pressed a finger against his mouth. "It's not that. It's…memories. Heightened emotions." A tear streaked her cheek, and he brushed it away with a thumb. "Guess I just need to release some of my emotions."

"You go right ahead and do it. Release away. Cry, yell, cuss. You can even hit me if it will make you feel better."

She laughed weakly and let a few more tears free. "You'd do that for me?"

He kissed her, more deeply this time. "Absolutely I would. I still owe you for coming to my rescue."

"You know you don't owe me, right?"

"Yes. The real reason I'm offering to listen and be your punching bag is because… You mean the world to me."

With her arms wrapped tight around his neck, she cried without feeling embarrassed or like she needed to hide her pain.

He's the comfort I've been needing.

Chapter Eleven

Nicholas held Emma while she cried in the middle of her daughter's nursery. No longer completely pink, it had become a magical room for any child. They swayed in a slow dance until her tears eased and her knees went weak as she sagged against him. Lifting her into his arms, he carried her to the guest room he'd been using and sat on the bed with her on his lap.

"Just let go and get it all out, honey. Cry as long and as hard as you want to. I'll never tell you that you can't cry." He hadn't been allowed such things, but he didn't want that for her. And he certainly didn't want his own child repressing his emotions. Jax would be encouraged to express his feelings appropriately to the situation, and hopefully Emma could teach them both what that looked like. Her tears had soaked his shirt, and he was surprised to discover his own cheeks were wet.

He was crying... And there was another person in the room. Nick let tears fall for Emma, for Aurora, for his son and himself. Emma was in his arms, trusting him with her pain in a time of weakness. The attraction and connection between them had become something almost tangible. He knew when she entered a room, and when she left, he looked forward to seeing her once again.

His longing ramped up, but it wasn't a need for sex that would only temporarily satisfy. It was bone-deep desire for Emma to be a permanent part of his life.

Are my feelings only lust induced by chemistry?

One soft brush of her hand against his could spark a fire. He longed for the addicting scent of her skin fresh from a shower or when she'd spent time in the sunshine. He nuzzled his cheek against her forehead and knew it was undeniably more than lust. It was the other *L* word that he couldn't remember ever saying to another person except his son. Jax had pulled the expression of love from him immediately. And possibly, his tiny son had taught him how to love.

"It was a car accident," she said in a whisper that was hoarse from crying.

It took Nicholas only a second to realize she was talking about how she'd lost her family. He'd never asked, but if she wanted to tell him he would not stop her. "I'm listening."

"A truck driver was texting… He ran a red light, and my world imploded."

Her grasp tightened on the front of his shirt, twisting and pulling until a button popped, but he didn't care if Emma ruined every shirt he owned. He'd wear dollar-store T-shirts if it meant making her happy. With her curves still fitted against his chest like they were tailored just for him, he lay on his back, and she settled along his side with her head resting on his shoulder.

Her hair was cool and soft beneath his fingers, and her arm across his chest made contentment settle in. "You don't have to talk about it if you don't want to."

"After such a big release of pent-up emotions and having you hold me through it, I want to. I want you to understand why I've been so guarded. It's just hard to know where to start."

"Take your time." He glanced at the clock on the bedside table and prayed Jax wouldn't wake up from his nap yet. "Will it help if I ask questions?"

"It might."

"How old was your daughter?"

"I was still pregnant. A week away from my due date."

His stomach hardened as nausea hit him, and he held her a little tighter.

"We were so happy and excited with a whole birth

plan ready to go. But it all changed in an instant. After the accident… I didn't want to live."

Nicholas caught his breath. The thought of never knowing her, of this world without her, was unthinkable.

"I was in the hospital for a week, and I refused to eat. But with the support of my family and friends—at first hour to hour and then one day at a time—I began to live again." Her voice caught, but she swallowed and tipped up her head to look at him. "You and Jax have helped me heal more than you realize."

He tucked her hair behind her ear. "I'm not going anywhere."

"Really?" she asked and looked him square in the eyes.

"Yes. Really."

Jax began to cry, and they smiled at one another. "I'll get him," they said in unison, then chuckled.

Together, they took a walk in the warm evening breeze, ate dinner, played with Jax and gave him a bath.

"Sweet baby boy, want to try out a new bed tonight?" Emma asked and kissed his cheeks until he giggled and churned his little legs like a bunny.

"I think that is an enthusiastic yes," Nicholas said. He kept a close eye on Emma as she walked through the open doorway of the nursery and took a seat in the rocking chair. There was no sign of tears. No trembling lip or chin. She looked beautiful and like a natural with a baby in her arms.

"I'm sorry, did you want to rock him?" she asked.

"No. Jax looks very happy to have you do it. His eyes are already closing." He leaned down, and she stopped rocking long enough for him to give each of them a quick kiss.

A few minutes later, Emma eased the baby onto the mattress, and in a position they'd grown fond of, he stood behind Emma with his arms around her waist and her fingers laced over his. They held on to one another until they were sure he'd stay asleep.

Taking Nick's hand, she led him from the room. "Feel like watching a movie?"

"Sounds good. Whose turn is it to pick the movie?"

"It's yours. Remember I made you watch the one about the secret princess?"

"Oh, yeah. How could I forget?" He had struggled to get through that one. "I'll check the movie channels and see what's on."

Emma fell asleep snuggled against him on the sofa, and even though it was an adventure movie he'd looked forward to, he watched her until the credits rolled.

"The movie is over," he said. She stretched, arching her body against his and setting off all kinds of sparks.

"Was it good?"

"I missed most of it, too. We can try again to-morrow night."

"Guess we should check on Jax and get some sleep." She stood and turned off the TV.

He followed her to the nursery where his son slept peacefully beneath the pastel sunrise, softly lit by a star-shaped nightlight. "Good night, my little man."

"Sweet dreams until sunbeams find you," she whispered.

Although Nicholas wanted to share a bed with Emma, he would not go into the space she'd shared with her husband without a very clear verbal invitation. He took a few heartbeats to calm himself and go through the list of why he needed to take things slow. A wounded heart still healing. A beautiful woman he respected…and loved.

At the doorway to her bedroom, he wrapped her in his arms, shivering when she ran both hands up his back to grip his shoulders. They swayed to a beat only they could hear, and her breath was warm against his neck.

"I'm right next door if you need me, sweetheart. For anything." He kissed her good-night, hoping she would come to him soon.

The minutes ticked by, but Emma was nowhere close to falling asleep. She had cried, found comfort and slept in Nick's arms, and now that the house was quiet and everyone was in bed, all she could think about was being held by him once again. Because Nick had made her take a look at her life, she'd recently spent a lot of time thinking about what was next for her.

Rolling to her side, she lifted the small photo album from her bedside table and flipped it open. A silvery puddle of moonlight illuminated Steven's image. A candid shot she'd taken at a backyard barbecue. He'd been laughing and telling a funny story about his game warden partner falling in a muddy creek while rescuing baby raccoons. It had been such a fun day.

"Nick said he isn't going anywhere, and he's there if I need him," she whispered. "It's so weird that I'm talking to you about this, but you were my best friend before you were my husband, and I really miss the way you listened. But you know what? It turns out Nick is a pretty good listener, too." She closed the album and put it away.

Finally in a place where she could acknowledge that Steven would expect her to keep living and move on, it was time to stop wasting opportunities.

No more holding myself back.

Emma got out of bed and crossed the hall to look in on baby Jax. The nursery was softly lit by the night-light, and he was still sleeping peacefully under the new sunrise mural. A rush of emotion tightened her throat, but it wasn't the overwhelming sadness of the past few years. It was tenderness, and a tentative joy she'd never thought she'd feel here again. It was such a relief to know this room wasn't forever locked in pain and sadness.

"I can remember the past while moving into the future," she whispered to the sleeping baby. "Sweet dreams until sunbeams find you, precious boy." She crossed to one of the windows and looked up at the stars. "Aurora, your baby boy is going to be okay."

She smoothed her midthigh cotton camisole nightgown. It wasn't sexy, but that's not why she was going to Nick. Not to seduce him, but to be close to his comfort and feel their connection. Nick's bedroom door was open so he could hear his son in the night, and she took it and his earlier offer of being there for her as an invitation and walked in, knowing exactly what she wanted. To be in his arms, whether they had sex or not. She just wanted to be held. But not by just anyone. By Nicholas Weller. The man she had wished would turn around and go back to Houston. The one she was now so thankful for.

In the shadowy darkness of the guest room, she could make out the line of his lower body under the white sheet. On his back with one long arm above his head, his chest was bared to the cool breeze of the ceiling fan. If she was an artist, she'd sketch or paint him just like this. A high voltage of attraction crackled through the air.

Maybe I do want more than to just be held.

She slipped under the sheet and slid her arm across his warm body.

Rolling toward her, he inhaled against her hair and a moan vibrated through his chest. "Em, are you okay?"

"If you're okay with me being here, then I'm more than all right." *Please, please be okay with this.*

"I've been waiting for you." Pulling her closer, he nuzzled his face against her neck.

Tension released from around her heart. Face-to-face and emboldened by his response to her slipping into his bed, Emma hooked her leg over his thigh, toned from running and whatever fabulous mixture of genes nature had seen fit to grace him with. "Sorry it took me so long. I let fear hold me back."

"What are you afraid of, honey?"

How did she explain what it felt like to have your world ripped away? Could anyone who'd never been through such a thing even begin to understand the soul-deep ache that could pull you under to a place no one should have to go? When she shivered, in a tender sweep of his fingers, he brushed her hair back from her face but didn't push for an answer. The warmth and strength of his body infused her with what she'd been missing. She let each breath relax her more and more and soaked in the amazing feeling of being close to someone in this way.

"Moving on," she whispered. "Experiencing more loss."

"Tell me what you need."

"You are already doing it."

He drew her leg higher on his hip, trailing his fingertips along the back of her thigh and making her arch against him. The increased pressure made sparkles swirl and dance through her blood.

His breath hissed on a quick inhale. "Do you need to talk some more?" The tone of his voice gave away his struggle to take things slow and delay his own pleasure.

She hadn't thought she could possibly be more attracted to Nicholas, but he'd found a way. He was holding back the desire that was physically evident against her while offering to listen if that's what she needed.

I can't believe I used to hope he'd leave town. I'm so glad I wasn't granted that wish.

"I think I'm all talked out. But if I haven't told you yet, you are a really good man."

"I don't hear that very often. Thank you." Running his hand up the center of her back, his fingers slipped into her hair, tipping her head to meet him eye to eye.

The tenderness in his gaze was mixed with a heat that she felt to her very core. An invitation to show her how good they could be together. "Yes. Yes, please," she said in answer to his silent question.

The corners of his mouth lifted into a devastatingly handsome smile, and his fingers massaged her scalp, making her shiver and moan. Giving her the courage to slip her hand between them, down along his chest and abdomen to skim the tips of her fingers beneath the waistband of his boxer briefs.

A low growl of pleasure rumbled in his chest and his hand flexed against her scalp, tugging her hair just enough to ignite a glowing ember in her very center. If he could bring this much pleasure with only his hand in her hair, what magical things awaited her?

Finally, his mouth settled firmly against hers. Soothing, seeking, lips caressing, tongue swirling with hers. His spicy scent and taste coursing through her.

"My sweet Em," he whispered against her ear.

"Show me how good we can be together. I need to feel alive."

He chuckled and flipped her onto her back. "We can do that. Hopefully in several different ways."

She giggled but then gasped in delight when he pressed his hips right where she needed him most. "I'm really liking that plan. I can't wait to see what you have in mind."

"Kiss me first," he whispered against her mouth.

She didn't make him ask again. They fell into a kiss that seemed to be accompanied by music, but it was their mingled moans and combined hearts racing to discover each other.

Nick eased the straps of her camisole from her

shoulders, sliding the nightie down her body and lingering to caress her breasts. "You are so lovely. So sweet. Tell me what you need."

"More. I need more of you. All of you." Impatient to be skin to skin, she undressed him and wrapped herself around his muscular body.

His talented hands and mouth sent sparkles swirling and dancing across her vision and straight to every place she needed him most. Heat licking her body, building and building into a night that she would remember even if she lived to be a hundred.

Even though there was one bottle to make in the night, Emma woke beside Nick in the guest room bed. She savored the warmth of his bare skin against hers, and while he was still asleep, she took the opportunity to admire the structured line of his jaw and the hint of morning stubble that made him look extra sexy. Her gaze lowered to his stomach, sculpted with a six-pack of muscles she wanted to kiss, again. A moment later, she realized his eyes were open and he was grinning at her.

"See anything you like?" he asked and rolled her onto her back.

"As a matter of fact, I do." Wrapping her legs around him, she trailed her fingers along his spine and smiled when a groan rumbled through his chest.

"Why don't you show me what it is that has you smiling?"

"Gladly."

They discovered several new ways to make the other one smile, and although they should be exhausted from a lack of sleep, they were full of energy.

After breakfast, they packed the diaper bag and loaded up in her car.

"Where are we going?" Nicholas asked.

"It's a surprise. Hey, you never told me how it went when you went car shopping the other day."

"They only had colors I didn't care for in stock, so I ordered a silver one. It will be a few weeks before it comes in."

Emma turned at the stop sign and slowed as they neared Cochran Blacksmithing. "And here it is."

"Oh, wow." He looked at her as if he couldn't figure her out. "You remembered me talking about my interest in blacksmithing."

"I did." And she couldn't stop adding new details to her daydreams of Nick striking hot metal with a large hammer, the clang of steel reverberating through the air and her bones. Muscles bunching in his arms and across his bare chest. And the fantasy was even better now that she had seen and explored every inch of his body. Suddenly burning up from the inside, Emma directed the air conditioner vent toward her heated face and parked beside a huge black motorcycle.

Daniel, the gentle-giant blacksmith, stepped out

of a large sliding metal door and waved a hand that could easily belong to a bear. He was tall and broad-shouldered with tribal tattoos and sun-bleached blond hair held back in a long braid. As rough and tough as he appeared, Emma knew he was more like a playful puppy.

The guys hit it off and got so deep in conversation that Emma was bored. She put the baby in the stroller and took Jax for a walk.

"Your daddy is working so hard to be the best father he can. But I won't lie. I was a little bit—okay, a lot—nervous at first, but he surprises me in good ways every day. And he loves you to pieces."

Jax stuck out his tongue and blew a raspberry while waving his arms, and it made her laugh. "You are such a good baby. Your uncle Marco is going to come see you this weekend so he can be at the gallery opening. And he is going to be so surprised at how much you have grown."

His baby babble sounded like he was really trying to tell her something, and she talked to him like they were having a real back-and-forth conversation.

When they returned to the blacksmith shop, it was another thirty minutes before the guys stopped talking about molten metal and fire and tools. She got a kick out of seeing Nicholas so excited and was glad she'd called Daniel and set up this meeting. Once they finally got into her car, Nicholas was all smiles, and she liked seeing him so happy.

"Thank you for setting this up for me. You've done more to encourage my interest than my own family ever has." He leaned over from the passenger seat and kissed her cheek, and when she turned toward him, they shared a deeper kiss.

"You are very welcome. I'm glad you made a new friend and have a playdate scheduled," she said with a big grin.

He barked out a quick laugh. "Do not go around town telling people I have a playdate with the blacksmith."

"It will be our little secret."

He turned up the air conditioner and made sure a back vent was directed toward Jax in the center of her back seat. "If you want to set up a playdate for Jax, that's a whole different story. Right, little man?" he said to his son.

Jax bunny-hopped his chubby legs and cooed.

She started the car and pulled out onto the road headed for the town square. "Tell me what you and Daniel have planned."

"I'm going to come back sometime after the gallery opening. Daniel said it's best if we start with a demonstration. Then I'll be able to see how he uses the tools and some of his techniques. After that, I'll probably try my hand at something simple first and see how it goes from there."

"Do I get to come and watch you forge some hot metal with a big hammer?"

"You want to watch me?"

"Maybe." The warmth of a blush made its way up her face and neck.

"Emma Blake, do you have a blacksmith fantasy? I need to hear more about this."

"It's possible that I might have thought about it a time or two."

He teased her and they laughed together until they got to the gallery and went inside to work on some of the final details for the opening. Getting everything done took longer than it should have because every time Jax fell asleep, they fell into one another and made out like teenagers.

The night of the gallery opening had arrived, and Weller's Art & Wine was finally ready to be introduced to the world. The original oak floors were varnished to a high sheen that made them gleam under the new lighting, but they had not been perfectly refinished. You could still see the character and history of the place in the scrapes and gouges from the years of use. The walls were a soft blue-gray that wouldn't interfere with the art. And for tonight's opening party, the space was extra sparkly with glistening crystal glasses, fresh flowers and candles scattered about among the artwork. Two bartenders and the caterers moved around, setting up the final touches that would make this evening perfect.

All of Nick's hard work had created a beautiful space that was ready for people to enjoy. Nan Curry's award-winning quilt hung on one wall flanked by two tall sculptures, one wooden and one bronze. Paintings of all sizes were artfully arranged on the walls above cases of jewelry, blown glass and even leather work. Music played softly and food—both attractive and delicious—was arranged on a table by the front windows.

Emma swished the full skirt of the new turquoise chiffon-and-silk dress Jenny had made for her, and she felt like a princess. But more than the pretty dress, it was Nick who made her feel like she was glowing. The memory of his touch from their afternoon shower still lingered on her skin, and the sweet and sexy things he whispered in her ear every time they made love echoed through her mind. She pressed her fingertips to her lips to hide the grin, worried people would be able to read her thoughts.

"I think everything is ready," Nick said from behind her.

Facing him, she smiled and slipped easily into his embrace. "It all looks amazing. And so do you." In her favorite light gray suit, he was as magnificent as the artwork.

"No one will be looking at the space or the art with you in the room. You outshine all of it."

"You are such a charmer."

Nicholas glanced at his watch. "People will start arriving anytime now."

"Is Jax still asleep?"

"Yes, but I'm sure he will wake up about the time the first guests arrive. Marco is in the office with him and has promised to keep an eye on him all evening. I think he has missed his nephew."

"I'm sure he has. I hope he knows he can call or visit anytime he wants."

"He does. He's going to need family as much as Jax." Nicholas took her by the hand and they walked through the space, admiring all the hard work. "I couldn't have done this without you."

"Oh, please. You could do this kind of thing in your sleep."

"Not true. At Weller's I had plenty of help with this kind of thing."

"Well, I was glad to help."

The front door opened, and the first guests arrived. Once the party was in full swing, Alexandra was set up in a corner with her acoustic guitar, singing in her beautiful, clear voice. And in an emerald green dress, she looked like a movie star.

Emma mingled and talked with everyone, proudly showing them around the gallery. It might not be her place, but it was certainly a nice addition to the Oak Hollow town square.

Nicholas stood by the front door of his gallery and let the moment soak in. He'd done it. He had created something of his own. He'd built a business and a life that made him happy and content. There was a twinge of guilt about not inviting his family, but he hadn't told them about Jax yet. That was on his agenda for next week, or maybe the one after that. This wasn't the first time he'd been accused of procrastinating, but he had a lot to think about.

The door opened and he turned to greet more guests. "Eric, Jenny so glad you could come tonight."

"We wouldn't have missed it," Eric said.

Nicholas kneeled in front of their daughter Lilly. She was using her little pink walker that Emma had said was called a gait trainer. "Hello, Lilly."

"Hi. Where's Jax?"

"He's in the back office with his uncle. I'll go and get him in a minute. He is going to be so happy to see you."

The little girl grinned. "We're friends."

"He's lucky to have such a good friend." He stood and shared a smile with her parents.

"Everything looks amazing," Jenny said.

"Eric and Christopher are the reason this place looks so great. Hiring your company was a good decision."

Jenny stood on her tiptoes to kiss her husband's cheek. "He is such a talented craftsman."

"Yes, he is. Please, grab a drink and some food and enjoy yourselves." As the family moved into the gallery, he thought how happy they looked together, then he caught Emma smiling at him from across the room. *Is that how we look to others?*

The gallery opening had been a huge success, and now Nicholas was tired but at the same time full of energy. He'd just gotten his son to sleep, Marco was upstairs in the garage apartment, and Emma was in the shower. When he went into the bathroom, she had her head tipped back as the spray of water rushed down the front of her shapely body.

She is so amazing. How did I get this lucky?

He thought he couldn't be more aroused, but he'd been wrong. His skin pulsed with a need to be close to her. Shucking off the rest of his clothes as fast as he could, he stepped in behind her.

"I was hoping you'd join me," she said and wrapped her arms around his neck, bringing their bodies together. "I need my back washed."

"Only your back?" His hands slid easily across her wet, soapy skin, flushed a pretty pink from the hot water.

"To start with."

The way she grinned, then bit her lower lip, made him growl and sink into a deep kiss. She smiled when he lathered his hands, but she moaned and sighed when he began to wash her whole body, slowly and thoroughly.

After the water had grown cold, they made their way to bed. "Sweet Em, I want to learn all the ways you like to be touched and kissed. I want to discover the secret sensitive places that make you moan in pleasure."

Straddling his hips, she rose above him, hazy beams of moonlight on one side of her body. When she leaned down to press her lips to his, her hair curtained down around them and consumed him in everything that was her. Soft skin, warm breath, sweet female sounds and her vanilla scent stealing his last bit of restraint. Everything about her captured his heart and mind and made his temperature rise faster than a bonfire.

I'll never get enough of this woman.

Chapter Twelve

While Nicholas was busy in a morning meeting with the gallery manager and employees, Emma took Jax with her and went to Green Forest Nursery. Today was the day of her annual trip to pick out trees in remembrance of Steven and Rose. This was something she liked to do on her own, but Jax was the perfect person to ease herself into sharing the tradition with someone. The baby wouldn't question her about any of it. Nick knew more than a lot of people about her pain and the grief she still carried, and she knew he'd support her, but this year's tree planting would double as a sort of "moving on" moment for her, and next year it could be something she'd share.

After she parked, she put the wiggly baby into the carrier on her chest, then walked the rows of plants. His bunny rabbit legs were going full speed as if he was hopping through the air. "I bet you're going to walk earlier than most." He looked up at her and hooted like a little owl, making her smile and her heart fill with happiness. "You are such a talker. I wonder what your first word will be?"

With one hand cradled around Jax in the carrier, she used the other to pull out trees until she found two that were perfect. A red oak for Steven and a crepe myrtle for Rose.

A young man with black hair held back in a low ponytail came toward her with a rolling flatbed cart. "I thought you might need this."

"Thanks. I do. Could you put these two trees on the cart?"

"Sure." He easily centered them on the flatbed. "If you want larger trees, we offer delivery and planting."

"Thanks for the offer, but I like to do it all myself. That's why I chose trees in the ten-gallon pots. I can handle them alone and they will fit lying down in the back of my SUV."

"Okay. Let me know if you need help." He picked up a misplaced plant and went down the row.

She pulled the cart up to the front with one hand, paid and let the same young man load them into her SUV. Jax fell asleep on the way home, and they got there before Nick. With his car seat sitting in the shade, she put the trees in the area where she would dig the holes tomorrow. She stood back to get a better look, and when she was satisfied with their placement, she carried the sleeping baby inside.

Nicholas arrived a few minutes later with lunch, and after they ate, he went outside to touch up some white paint on the garage while she got to work on the weekly bookkeeping for the shop.

A couple of hours later, Emma eased the empty bottle from the sleeping baby's mouth and wiped a dribble of milk from his chin. "You are so precious. I love you, sweet boy." It felt so good to let herself love again.

As soon as she put Jax down for a nap in the nursery, she'd go outside and see what had kept Nick so busy for the last few hours. Just as she rose from the sofa, the doorbell rang, and with a sleeping baby in the crook of one arm, she looked through the peephole.

A gentleman with salt-and-pepper hair and a fancy suit and tie stood beside a beautiful woman in a colorful Gucci dress Emma had recently seen in a magazine. The older couple on her front stoop were no one she'd ever met, yet something about the man was familiar. He rubbed his chin while staring upward, in a way Nicholas frequently did, and Emma's heart slammed against her ribs.

Nooo! Are they his parents?

She smoothed her hair, pasted on a smile and opened the door. "Good afternoon. How can I help you?"

"I am Juliana Weller, and this is my husband, Franklin Weller," said the woman in a very proper but not unkind tone of voice. "We are Nicholas Weller's parents and were told this is where he lives."

Oh, shoot. I was right.

"Yes, it is. Please, come in." She stepped aside and they walked past her into her entryway. They'd only glanced at the infant in her arms, but since Nicholas hadn't told them, they had no idea he was their grandchild. "So nice to meet you. I'm Emma Blake. Is Nicholas expecting you?"

"No, he's not," Franklin Weller said, and not so subtly glanced around her entryway and living room. "I told you our son would rent a nice place."

They think this is his place? Emma opened her mouth to correct them, but snapped it closed. He *had* been paying rent, and without her even realizing it... Her house kind of had become his place, too. He hadn't slept in the apartment in over a month. And neither of them had been sleeping alone. She put a hand to her cheek, hoping the warmth wasn't showing as a bright red blush.

"You must be our grandson's nanny?" Franklin said.

So, they do know Jax is their grandchild.

How had they found out? Had Nick told them and

not mentioned it? "I'm not a nanny. Please, come have a seat." She led them to the sofa but remained standing while gently swaying to keep Jax asleep.

"I guess you call it babysitting here in a small town?" Juliana asked as she sat beside her husband.

Emma forced herself to resist a major eye roll. "We have both nannies and babysitters in Oak Hollow, but I'm neither." She had no idea what to call herself in front of them.

"So, you are…a friend?"

"Yes, ma'am." Afraid of stirring up unnecessary trouble, Emma decided to give them as little information as possible. "Would you like to hold your grandson while I get you something to drink?" *And go find your son.*

There was a hesitation as they both studied the baby in her arms. "Not right now," Mrs. Weller said. "I'm wearing silk."

Wow. Nick wasn't kidding. Disappointment on behalf of Nick and Jax brought a lump to her throat. Her parents wouldn't have gotten through the doorway before wanting to hold their grandchild.

"Where is our son?" His father asked and glanced at his watch. "We are here to take them home."

It felt as if all the air had been sucked out of the room. *Home? Isn't Oak Hollow their home now?* She held Jax a little tighter and couldn't stop herself from questioning this idea. "You're taking them home for a visit?" Maybe they had just come to pick them up since Nick's car wasn't suitable for a car seat.

"Nicholas will be moving back to Houston now. Returning and running Wellers has always been the plan."

Her legs went numb, and she sat in the chair behind her. "I didn't know."

Nick had never given her any impression that he intended to leave Oak Hollow. In fact, it was the opposite. When he'd first moved into her garage apartment, he'd talked about looking for a house. He'd just opened his gallery. He was living with her as if they were a couple. A family. And the night they made love for the first time, he'd said he wasn't going anywhere.

Every cell in her body throbbed painfully and threatened to implode. Too many strong emotions crowded forward all at once. Surprise, confusion, hurt and anger. Her blood was rushing too fast, and her head was beginning to pound.

This can't be right. What is happening?

Mr. Weller cleared his throat and raised a gray eyebrow. "Ms. Blake, where is our son?"

"I think he's in the garage. I'll go get him."

"What is it with that boy and his cars and garages?" Franklin said to his wife.

Before Emma could make her legs work enough to stand and support her weight, the kitchen door opened, then closed with a slight bang that made her flinch.

"Em, come see—" Nicholas broke off speaking and halted midstride, staring through the pass-through from the kitchen. "Mother. Father. What are you doing here?"

"We are here to take you and our grandson home, of course." His father stood and buttoned his suit coat. "It's time."

Emma also stood and put a few feet of distance between herself and his parents. She cradled a hand around Jax's head and lifted him to nuzzle her cheek against his downy hair, inhaling his scent and praying Nick would laugh and then send them home after a short visit. She wanted to shout that he'd made friends and built a successful business here in Oak Hollow, and that there had to be some mistake because Nick and Jax were home. But her throat went as dry as desert sand, and her heart was in danger of shriveling and dropping into the pit of her stomach.

She looked at Nicholas while standing on the precipice of that dark place she'd worked so hard to crawl out of. She wanted to give him the benefit of the doubt, but he wouldn't meet her eyes.

Look at me, Nick. See me and tell me there's been some mistake and you haven't been planning to leave this whole time.

Nicholas squeezed his eyes closed and inhaled in a way she'd learned he did when he was trying to decide what to say. "How did you find out about my son?"

"Well, it certainly wasn't from you, like it should have been," his mother snapped, and this time her tone struck like a whip.

"I'm sorry about that," Nicholas said and turned on the water at the kitchen sink.

"We saw Philip Deco's parents at an event," she said. "They mentioned you coming out to the winery with your baby. Can you imagine our shock and difficulty pretending as if we already knew? You put us in quite the uncomfortable position, son. The second we could get away, we had Sara make a reservation at a B and B and pack overnight bags for us, and then we drove straight here."

Emma's gaze flicked between the three of them. Was Nick avoiding eye contact because he'd been keeping something from her or because he was as surprised as she was by their arrival?

Nicholas dried his hands and joined them in the living room. "I was planning to tell you, but…"

"This is a conversation we should not be having in front of your babysitter," his father said with a quick glance in Emma's direction.

She flinched, then focused on Jax when he squirmed in her arms.

"She's not my babysitter."

She waited for Nick to say more. Waited for him to say she was his girlfriend or at least that they were dating, but he just stood there staring at a spot on the ceiling as he braced his hands on the high-back chair. His demeanor wasn't giving her much hope. And her heart broke a little more.

"I'm going to take a walk," she said.

They remained silent and unmoving as she kissed the baby once more and then put him in the bassinet by the windows. Barely remembering to slip on her flip-flops, she rushed out the front door.

"I should have known something like this would happen." She'd told him keeping his parents in the dark was a bad idea. But worse than that, she should have realized that Nick would eventually go back to his original life. Back to his multigenerational family business and the responsibilities he'd been groomed for since birth.

Her entire body trembled, and her feet were too numb to care what surface she was striking with each step. Emma walked and walked, weaving down one street and up another, paying little attention to where she was going, but found herself at the gate of the cemetery. It was a place she didn't often visit. Where others found comfort here, it wasn't that way for her and only made her sadder. Her own backyard was where she felt closest to her family.

"That's where I need to be." She spun around and started on the quickest route home. She'd sit beside the six trees and prepare herself to plant the two new ones tomorrow. Another wave of sorrow made her stumble. She had hoped having Nick and Jax in her life would make this anniversary a little easier to bear, but now, she'd plant the trees for the two she'd lost years ago while carrying a new layer of sadness for the two currently slipping through her fingers.

"What was I thinking?" she whispered to herself and stepped over a crack in the sidewalk. "I should've listened to my initial gut reaction when I first met Nicholas. I never should have allowed myself to get this close to them. Letting myself love them was stupid." At least she had been smart enough not to involve Nicholas in her special tree-planting tradition.

Emma worked herself up to a point where her emotions shut down and all she could feel was numb both inside and out. She would have to deal with the hurt later, but right now, she just needed to get through what came next. It was time for a hard conversation with Nick.

Am I going to have to let go of another man and child?

Chapter Thirteen

Nicholas hated being ambushed, especially by Franklin and Juliana Weller.

He sat across from his parents, and as hard as his own procrastination had bitten him in the ass, it was a wonder he could sit down at all. But his anger about them paying Aurora to leave him had not faded and thinking about what he would someday have to say to his son about his mother had only added to the emotion. He glanced over his shoulder at Jax, sleeping peacefully and unaware of the turmoil. Pressure built up inside him, and he bit the inside of his cheek. Without warning, it was coming to a head, and he'd have to overcome his tendency to go quiet when he was confronted with a negative emotion. *I need to think before saying anything I'll regret.*

"Your baby is very cute," his mother said.

"Yes, he is."

"Tell us how this happened." His father's voice held the usual demanding quality that had set Nicholas's teeth on edge for years. "Who is the mother?"

"Aurora Di Ciano." His parents shared a look that made his skin prickle. It was no doubt a reaction to their decision to use money to get their way, but Nicholas wasn't going to be the one to say it. "She never told me she was pregnant. Her brother said she didn't know until after..." He gave them a hard stare. "After she unexpectedly left me."

"I knew she wasn't right for you," his father said. "Where is she now?"

So, they aren't going to fess up.

He pressed his thumbs to the underside of his brow bones and reminded himself that losing his cool would not help the situation, and although it sure would feel good, he was too tired to escalate things by yelling. Soaking in a little guilt might do them some good. "She died the day after she gave birth."

His mother clasped a hand against her mouth. "Oh, that's terrible. I'm sorry, son. But are you sure the baby is yours?"

Only she could turn sympathy into blame in the same breath. "Yes, I'm sure."

His father stood and began pacing. "Did you get a DNA test?"

"I did. He's mine. His name is Nicholas Jackson Weller, but we call him Jax."

"We?" she asked.

"Me and Emma."

Her eyes narrowed on him. "Is there something more going on between you two?"

"Yes. She was a friend who helped me when I needed it most, and now she is my girlfriend."

"You should have told us about the baby right away and come straight home," his mother said, conveniently dismissing what he'd said about Emma.

As well as the fact that he was a grown-ass man. "I'm not a teenager and haven't been for a long time, Mother. I needed to figure a few things out before telling you."

His father crossed the room and back again. "Is this her house?"

"It is."

"What does she do for a living?" he asked.

"She's a teacher and small-business owner."

"What kind of business does—"

Juliana caught hold of her husband's arm as he walked by. "It doesn't matter," she said. "And sit down. You are making me nervous with your incessant pacing."

"I just want to know who our son has been cohabitating with."

Nicholas dropped his head into his hands. He knew better than to get in between them when they got started. Not unless he wanted to escalate things further by dragging this into the territory of feuding spouses.

"It doesn't matter because Nicholas will be back home where he has belonged *this whole time*." His mother's last three words were said with extra emphasis and a sharp glare for her husband.

It sounded as if she had not been on board with the whole idea of sending him off to prove himself. While his parents bickered, Nick's initial surprise was wearing off… And Emma's face flashed before him. All he wanted to do was talk to her about this. She had a way of calming him and making him see things in a new way. He sat forward on the edge of his chair, poised to go find the woman who'd stolen his heart, but Jax was asleep, and he couldn't leave him with his parents.

How sad is that when I can't leave my baby with his own grandparents?

"Nicholas, I know you weren't scheduled to come back to Houston yet, but we need you to come home now," he said.

"Scheduled? I didn't know there was a schedule." Unable to sit still, Nicholas began to pace just like his father had done. "I wasn't given the manual for this little experiment of yours."

Franklin stiffened and adjusted a tie that was already perfectly straight. "My father did this same thing to me. Call it a tradition before taking the reins."

Anger rattled behind Nick's rib cage. Once upon a time he'd wanted nothing more than to be the fourth generation of Wellers to run the prestigious auction house. But in this moment… For all he cared, his sister could take over. She was more business focused anyway and honestly better at it than him.

His mother stood and stepped in front of him. "The timing of you being away actually works out perfectly."

"The timing?" He took a step back and sat down.

"Yes," she said. "We will say you eloped with the mother and then she died in childbirth. Hopefully the death will make people overlook the fact that she would've been pregnant before you married."

"Excellent plan," his father said.

A tight, painful band threatened to crush his ribs. "You can't be serious?" They were talking like this had really happened and wasn't a scheming concoction from their imaginations to protect the family image.

His mother folded her hands in her lap like she always did when she found a conversation distasteful. "It will never be known that the baby was born out of wedlock."

"Are you kidding me? You want to use Aurora's

death to save your name?" Nicholas said through gritted teeth.

"*Our* name. It's the only way," his father said. "You made the mistake and have to pay a price for that, son."

Red flashed before his eyes, and Nicholas sprang to his feet. "My mistakes? Pay the price? This is all on you, old man." He jabbed a finger toward his father, who looked thoroughly taken aback. "I know about the payoff. If you hadn't driven the pregnant mother of my child away, we would've gotten married for real. My son would have been born to married parents."

And if I'd been at the hospital, maybe I could've saved her.

"That's enough," his mother said with an uncharacteristically raised voice. "That was in the past. All that matters now is getting you and our grandson home."

"The one you haven't even asked to hold? We are happy here with Emma. She is—"

"Nicholas!" His mother stood ramrod straight. "You can't be serious. You want to stay here because you believe you are in love with some small-town girl?"

"That's enough, Mother. Emma is a smart, successful woman and I love her." Saying *I love you* out loud was not something his family did, and his parents' eyes widened.

"Son, think," his father said. "Are you sure she's not after money or a new life in Houston?"

"Emma is not after my money. She has her own, and she is happy here with a home and business she loves." His voice sounded emotionless even though on the inside he was furious.

Franklin Weller lifted his glasses to rub his eyes. "Just because she likes it here, you can't actually consider staying in this town long term."

"Everything is up for consideration."

His mother crossed the room to the bassinet and looked at the baby, an unreadable expression on her face. Jax was a sound sleeper, but he must really be tired to sleep through this conversation.

With a long sigh, Franklin started pacing again. "If you are serious about this woman, ask her to come with you. The house is certainly big enough, and she seems to be good with the baby. You deserve more than what you can find here."

Nicholas barked a quick laugh. "You haven't even asked what I've found here. You aren't curious about my art gallery and wine bar?"

"You're right, son," he said. "We stopped there first and that's how we found out where you live. It's a very nice gallery. We should have started by congratulating you."

Wow. A congratulations as if he were an acquaintance, but not the interest you might give a son. With each thing his parents said, they were ticking off another box on his list of reasons to stay in Oak Hollow.

"Your success here is proof you have the drive and determination. And that's another reason I need you back at Weller's."

He suddenly couldn't bear the thought of going back to their world. The world that was once his and all that he'd ever known. But now, Nicholas recognized it as a stifling version of what life could be. In this small town with his amazing woman, he was truly content for the first time in his life and that was worth fighting for.

His mother spun around and rejoined the discussion. "You should start packing while your father and I go back to our room at the B and B. We can leave first thing in the morning."

"I will not be joining you tomorrow."

She glared at Franklin when he started to speak. "I suppose it makes sense that you'll need more time to close things up here before returning to Houston. When do you think you'll be home?"

He looked them square in the eyes. "I don't know that I will return to Houston for more than a visit." Their astonished expressions were almost comical, and if the whole situation wasn't so pathetic, he would have laughed. "I have a lot to think about."

"We've all gotten ourselves worked up," she said. "Nicholas, we can talk more later and when the baby is awake, we can have a proper introduction to our grandson."

At least she is acknowledging she has a grand-child.

When Emma got home, his parents' silver Jaguar was still in front of her house. If Nick decided to stay... She sucked in a sharp breath.

No! I can't let myself hope for that.

Even if Nick and Jax didn't leave today or tomorrow, it was probably Nick would eventually miss his old lifestyle and leave at some point. Her blood was rushing too fast, and she clasped the sides of her pounding head. He hadn't found it important enough to tell her he was expected to return to Houston and run the family business. Why had he kept this from her?

Was I just a temporary replacement mom and lover?

She went down the driveway to the backyard but paused in confusion beside her car. Two empty ten-gallon pots sat in front of the garage.

She gasped. "What happened to my new trees?" With panic setting in, she turned in a circle, and when she saw them, something cold pierced her heart.

"No! No, no, no. He planted my trees."

With a block of ice in her chest, she rushed forward and dropped to her knees in front of them. Her vision dimmed and wavered as she flashed back to the moments right before the car accident. A dark place in her memory she tried never to go.

They had been driving home from dinner with her family, and because of all the food she'd eaten, her baby was moving like a break dancer. She had her hand on her belly savoring the magical movement of tiny hands and feet and knees creating unusual bumps on her stomach. Steven was driving and singing off-key to a country song, and she was talking to her unborn baby girl, apologizing for her father's singing and making him laugh. Her world had been beautiful and perfect. So much love and so much to look forward to.

And then…

A burst of gripping fear, a metallic crunch followed by a sickening feeling of weightlessness, and then everything fading to black. Her first awareness was ringing in her ears, followed by the distant, muffled sound of voices and sirens. Searing pain sending her in and out of consciousness, fear mounting each time she came to awareness. Calling out for Steven with each painful breath.

Emma whimpered and squeezed a fistful of freshly turned dirt at the base of Rose's tree as phantom pain radiated through her muscles. Tears flowed down her face and a sharp stick bit into her flesh. Tomorrow's tradition honoring her family had been ruined. The trees were in their places, but she hadn't been the one to plant them. And it was one day too soon, but ripping them out of the ground just to replant them felt wrong. The deed was done.

"I can't ever go through anything like the accident again. It would kill me," she said in a hoarse voice unfamiliar to her own ears. She knew there was something real between her and Nick, even if he didn't love her the way she'd hoped, but if Nick and Jax stayed, she would fall even deeper in love. And if something were to happen to one of them or if he decided to stay only to leave at a later date, she might not survive it. At least with them in Houston, she could imagine them living a happy healthy life.

She should have realized that there was no way he wouldn't eventually go back to the family business. She'd been a fool to think otherwise. Now, she just had to stay strong and not allow Nicholas to change her mind.

"It has to be over. I have to end our relationship."

Chapter Fourteen

Nicholas was about to put the baby into the stroller and go look for Emma when she came in through the kitchen door. She was pale and trembling with smudges of dirt on tear-streaked cheeks.

"Em, what happened? Are you okay?" When he rushed toward her, she backed away with her arms wrapped around her middle. The blankness of her expression made his stomach knot up.

"You planted my trees. The trees I bought for my special tradition to honor Steven and Rose." Her voice broke on the last word, and she covered her mouth.

"Oh, honey, I'm so sorry. I didn't know." He

came forward with his arms open wanting to comfort her, but she stepped back, again, bumping into the kitchen table.

"Don't, please." She held up a hand in a stay back motion.

"I was only trying to help and never meant to mess anything up for you. I'd never do that on purpose."

"I can't do this anymore."

"You can't do what?" Don't say it. Please, don't say it.

"This." She motioned between them. "Us."

He'd thought this crappy day couldn't get much worse, but his gut twisted into a tighter tangle of knots. "Is it my parents? I'm so sorry they ambushed you like that. What did they say to you?"

"It's not just them or the trees. Have you ever lost someone you loved so much that it feels like a part of you is missing?"

"Not yet." But he had a feeling he was about to.

"Going on without them seems impossible. They were your whole world. And now my world is divided into before and after, and I'm a different person. People say move on, but I haven't been ready."

"What can I do to help you, honey?" He wanted so badly to hold her close.

"Nothing. I can't face that kind of loss or pain again. I let myself get wrapped up in pretend, but it's not real," she said.

"Not real?" Another wave of fire hit his gut. "What have we been doing? Playing house? Make-believe?"

She clenched her hands. "Yes. That's exactly what we've been doing."

She needs to know it's real for me. "I—"

"Nick, listen to me. I've taught you all I can, and you're an amazing father. You should go back to Houston with your family. Go back to the auction house like you were meant to do."

When his jaw dropped open and he blinked rapidly, she squeezed her eyes closed as if she couldn't bear to see him. "You want me to leave Oak Hollow? You want us to go?"

Say no. Please say this is some sort of mistake and you want us to stay. Tell me you love me.

"It's too soon. I'm not ready and I pushed myself. I can't replace my family with you and Jax."

"I wouldn't expect you to. I would never try to replace them."

"You have a multigenerational family empire to take over. Your gallery manager and employees are great and can handle things here. You belong in Houston, and I belong here. But we don't belong together."

Déjà vu made his heart lurch against his breastbone. *We don't belong together.* The same words Aurora had said the day she dumped him without any warning. He'd walked away from that relationship with wounded pride, but now...

He'd never expected Emma to do the same thing. He was shredded.

Nicholas snapped into self-protect mode. She wasn't kidding. She wasn't going to take back what she was saying. Emma was suddenly and coldly ending their relationship. Another woman deciding he wasn't a forever guy. It was time to drag his sorry ass out of her life and back to his old one. "That's truly how you feel? Baby lessons are officially over, and we're done?"

"Yes." She shivered and rubbed her arms. "I let myself get caught up in everything. And I shouldn't have. I'm sorry."

A gaping hole opened in his chest and his insides turned to ash. "I see." He didn't understand, but he'd move on once again.

"I'll never forget our time together." She looked at her feet. "It's been wonderful. I'm going to say goodbye to Jax." Her voice quavered. "And then I think it's best if I go over to my parents' house for a couple of nights. That should give you time to pack. Dragging this out will only make it harder for all of us." She met his eyes briefly. "Just because we are ending things doesn't mean you aren't one of the best men I've ever known."

A lot of good that does me. Not trusting himself

to speak, he nodded and turned to walk away from the life he'd been so excited to build.

Emma stepped into the hallway bathroom and cringed at her disheveled appearance. With dirt on her face and hands, she was a total mess. After cleaning herself up, she went into the nursery and found Jax awake in the baby bed playing with his favorite toy—his toes.

"Hello, sweetie. How about a fresh diaper?"

Jax reached for her, and her heart broke a little more as she lifted him into her arms and hugged him tight. He grabbed a handful of her hair when she put him on the changing table, and she covered his cheeks with kisses. His precious baby giggle was one of the sweetest sounds on earth. A tear caught in her lashes then slowly trickled down her cheek. Emma took a minute to memorize his cherub face. His tiny fingers and toes. Thick lashes that would be the envy of every girl.

"You have gotten so big. You're almost ready for the next size of diaper." Who was going to tell Nick these kinds of things now? Her resolve to end things wavered, but she had to stay strong. This was the best option for the long run.

With a clean baby in her arms, she sat in the rocking chair. "I love you, sweet boy. And I will never ever forget you or your daddy. He is going to take good care of you because he loves you, too."

The baby cooed and wrapped his tiny fingers around one of hers.

"You've taught me I can still love, but that it's... Too risky." Her voice broke on the words and her throat burned.

Jax started fussing in a way that meant he was hungry, and his daddy appeared at the doorway of the nursery. At the sight of Nick with a bottle and a tortured expression, her chest constricted. She kissed each of Jax's little cheeks, stood and handed the baby to him but stepped away before Nick could touch her. If he did, she might break and beg him to stay. "I'm sorry things worked out like this."

"Me, too." He turned and left the room with the baby peeking at her over his shoulder.

Emma made herself walk out of the nursery and close the door. Maybe she'd seal it and never open it again. She shoved a few things into a duffel bag and then drove toward her parents' house.

When she'd first gone inside her house after discovering he'd planted the trees, Nick had opened his arms, and she'd wanted nothing more than to fall into his comfort, but she had to stay strong.

Emma thumped the steering wheel with one fist. "You had me believing you were building a life here. With me." This pain was nothing compared to what she'd been through, but it still sucked. Big-time.

Once she locked herself inside her childhood home, the strongest urge was to just give up and disappear into nothingness. The most she could make herself do was text Jenny that she'd broken up with Nick and wouldn't be coming to the shop the next day, before taking off her clothes and climbing into bed. Glow-in-the-dark stars swirled across the ceiling of the room she'd grown up in. As a child, she'd loved falling asleep beneath them, but now, they only made her think of dancing under the stars at the wedding with Nick. Evening turned to night and her heart retreated into the shadows. She lay motionless for so long that she fell asleep only to wake frequently from strange dreams and tears on her cheeks.

Nicholas thought briefly about moving back to the hotel on the edge of town and taking his time deciding what to do, just in case Emma changed her mind. But he couldn't properly take care of a baby in a hotel room. And he couldn't risk Jax getting too attached to Emma and then losing her. He had to protect his son from the pain he was currently feeling. That's what daddies were supposed to do. Back to Houston was the only place he knew to go.

Once he had hastily packed the essentials that would fit in his car, and between feeding and diapering, he took apart the infant high chair and baby swing and boxed up what he would have to ship to Houston. It was like a game of *Tetris* getting as much as possible into the trunk of his car. If it was just him, he would drive tonight, but with his son, who would be strapped in the front seat of his Corvette, he couldn't drive when he was tired.

"I should've just bought the black SUV instead of being so picky and ordering the silver one."

Sitting in the rocking chair in the nursery, Nick held Jax in front of him, cradled between his arms with the baby's head resting in the palms of his hands. Big trusting brown eyes counted on him to be a good daddy. His little feet kicked against his chest, the same ones that would grow and run and someday be as big as his. His son was the most precious thing in the world.

"Well, little man, I screwed up and it's just you and me, for real this time. We might not have our Emma…" Thickness clogged his throat.

She doesn't want to be my anything. She wasn't ready and I pushed her too far too fast.

He'd misjudged the whole situation. He'd thought they had fallen in love, but apparently, it was only him. Obviously, he had no idea what was in the minds of women.

"We'll be okay."

Jax whimpered and his lower lip poked out and quivered.

"Oh, sweet boy. Don't cry. You'll always have me." He kissed his son's forehead and hugged his tiny body to his aching heart. "I'm not going to hand you off to be raised by other people like I was. I promise. I'll see you every day, and we'll play and read books like you did with Emma." His breath caught again at the sound of her name.

Damn it. I can't stop thinking about her as being part of our lives.

"I won't let you grow up thinking you aren't one hundred percent wanted and loved for who you are."

If only there was a woman who truly wanted him.

The following day, with a bruised heart and ego, Nicholas moved back into his parents' mansion. What had once been his home now felt like a grand hotel with generic furnishings. Even though they sold antiques at the auction house, his suite contained no old record player and collection of albums that had belonged to his grandparents. There were no pieces of driftwood or pebbles from vacations lining the shelves with books and photos.

When his parents asked what had changed his mind about coming home, he vaguely hinted at family obligation. Thankfully that was enough for them, and he slid back into his old life—now as ill-fitting as someone else's shoes. In a matter of months, he had become a guest in his old life. He would throw himself into being a father and find a balance between parenting and working at Weller's.

Since Jax was getting too big for his bassinet, he pulled his king-size mattress off the frame and into a corner, tucking it flush against two walls. Like Emma and the baby book had taught him, he made sure there would be no pillow or anything his son could get tangled in. He would sleep near him and keep him safe through the night. Tomorrow the baby bed he'd ordered would be delivered, and he'd set a nursery up in the second bedroom of his suite.

Even though his suite was bigger than the garage apartment, he felt stifled, and he'd only been home a matter of hours. Nicholas put together and carried the infant high chair into the family dining room. He had a pretty good idea how this was going to go over, but he didn't feel a bit guilty about testing his parents. He was also testing himself to see if he could once again live in the same house. If they hadn't shown up in Oak Hollow and freaked Emma out, he might still be…

No, I can't keep doing this to myself.

His sister, Victoria, walked into the dining room. "Hello, baby brother. Welcome home."

He used to hate it when she called him that, but for the first time it didn't bother him. "Hey, Vic. How have things been around here?"

"About the same, other than Thomas moving out." She pulled out a chair, took off her high heels and pulled a clip from her hair. Shoulder-length brown curls tumbled around her cheeks.

He'd never liked his brother-in-law and was not sad to see him go, but he was sad for his sister. "I'm sorry it didn't work out."

She shrugged. "It's not much of a loss. Honestly,

it was more of a business match than a love match. Is that a high chair?"

"Yes. It converts to different positions as he grows."

She grinned and crossed her arms over her chest. "You do know how this is going to go over with the parental duo, right?"

He took a seat across from her and couldn't stop his own mischievous grin. "I have a pretty good idea."

Victoria laughed. "You always have liked to push their buttons."

"He's my son, and I get to decide how he is raised. They'll have to get used to having a baby in the house again, and if not, Jax and I will eat in the kitchen with the staff."

She smiled but there was sadness in her eyes. "This will be fun. Where is the little guy? I really want to meet my nephew."

Nicholas unclipped the video baby monitor from his belt and showed her the image of his sleeping baby. "He's napping. Walk with me and we'll go get him."

Victoria grabbed her designer shoes with the red leather soles and followed him out of the room and down the wide hallway to the east wing. Jax was kicking his legs and waking up when they walked in.

"Do you want to hold him?"

"I would love to."

He scooped up his son and kissed his cheek. "Hello, my little man. Let me change his diaper before you hold him."

"He is adorable. He looks like you but with darker hair and eyes."

Jax stuck out his tongue and blew a raspberry.

She laughed. "He's definitely your son. This is something I never thought I'd see. The ladies' man changing a diaper like a pro."

"I had a good teacher." His stomach clenched like it did every time he thought of Emma.

His sister sat in the chair beside his bed and held out her arms. "Let me squeeze this baby boy." Jax willingly went to her. "Hello there, cutie pie. I'm your aunt Victoria, but Vic might be easier for you to say"

He liked seeing his sister like this. Why hadn't he known this side of her? Before it had been all work and seriousness. "Neither Mother or Father have held him yet."

She sighed and let Jax shake her finger. "Sometimes I don't understand them. Babies are wonderful. I guess some people just aren't meant to be parents."

"I had no idea you liked babies. You never wanted to have one of your own?"

"I tried, but it just never happened for me." She gave a small shake of her head as if the subject was painful and changed the topic. "You aren't happy to be back in Houston."

"What makes you say that?"

"We might not have been that close growing up, but I do know you, and I can see the sadness."

He thought he was doing a good job of hiding his feelings the way he'd been taught to. Had his parents told her about Emma? "What did you hear?"

"Not much, other than you were coming home with your son, which was a huge shock. I'm so sorry to hear about Aurora."

"Thanks. I don't suppose they told you why I had no idea she was pregnant?" He clenched his jaw.

"No."

Nicholas told her the whole tragic story, and she was as angry as he was. They also talked about Emma until Jax fussed for a bottle and then made their way to the kitchen. He mixed up a small bowl of rice cereal and they took it with them to the family dining room. When their parents joined them a few minutes later, they barely contained their laughter at the expressions on Franklin and Juliana Weller's faces as they stared at the high chair like it was a foreign object. A baby at the dinner table was not something they were used to.

The best part of the meal was when Jax spit a mouthful of baby cereal and banged the tray of his high chair while squealing.

The next day, he reluctantly left Jax with the nanny his mother had hired and went to the auction house. He needed to find his place and his groove once again, but today had not been that day. He was exhausted from a mostly sleepless night of watching Jax sleep, and almost crying when the baby did, knowing his son was probably missing Emma as much as he was. He missed her teasing, her laugh, her kisses. He missed the warmth of her body beside him in bed.

It had been foolish of him to fall in love.

Chapter Fifteen

After a couple of mostly sleepless nights at her parents' house, Emma returned to hers. It was empty, just as she'd requested. And it sucked big-time. Nicholas Weller was gone from her life without putting up a fight, and that told her she'd made the right decision in ending it. If she ever had a relationship again, it had to be with someone who would fight for her. She turned away calls and visits from friends, telling everyone she just needed some time alone, and a week off work.

Emma stood at the door of the nursery and ignored her own warning not to go in and torture herself. Gloomy evening light filtered through the

blinds, dimming the magical and full-of-hope sunrise. She sat on the floor in the middle of the newly
remodeled nursery and made no attempt to stop the
big silent tears. She had to resist the urge to completely disappear into herself, because this time she
might stay there. But a brief visit to sorrow town
was called for.

After a trip to the bathroom, where she'd stared
into the mirror at her tangled hair and generally hag-
gard appearance, she decided against a shower because it would take too much energy. Back in her
bedroom, she pulled the covers over her head. Steven had been wrong about something good coming
out of the worst things.

She once again drifted into confusing dreams that
woke her frequently. The scent of evergreen came
to her as it always did when she dreamed of Steven. He was sitting beside her, stroking her head
and humming.

"Be happy, Bunny Rabbit. Grab every happiness.
Take my love with you and love again."

His image shimmered, and she grasped for him.
"Don't go. Please don't go. I don't know how to do
this."

"Yes, you do." He lightly touched the spot over
Emma's heart. Warmth spread and the weight of
sorrow eased a bit. His voice faded along with his
image.

She woke with his words ringing in her head.

Take my love with you and love again. Was it all in her imagination or was he truly visiting her dreams?

The next time she fell asleep, she briefly saw Steven holding out a blue envelope and telling her to read it. Then her dream changed to a sunny day. The weight of a baby in her arms. The spicy scent of the new man who had found his way into her life. The warmth of sunshine. A cool breeze on her skin. And she got lost in Nick's gaze.

Her heart had made room for someone else.

Emma sat bolt upright in bed, breath heaving and heart thrumming like a hummingbird. "The letter he left for me. That's what he wants me to read." She untangled herself from twisted bedsheets and got the blue envelope out of the back of her top dresser drawer. Steven had written it a year before his death and given it to his best friend and game warden partner to pass along to her if it was ever needed.

She'd only read the letter once then put it away because she hadn't been able to even think about such things as moving on. With the blue envelope clutched against her chest, she took it outside and sat beside the newly planted trees. Although she hadn't done the planting herself, she had picked them out and bought them, and without her saying a word, Nick had put them in the exact right spots. If everything both good and bad really did have a purpose like Steven believed, then maybe Nick's having a hand in this year's tradition was supposed to happen.

The morning sunlight was warm on her skin as she read Steven's words about wanting her to keep living and to love again. Grabbing every moment of happiness. Finding joy in every day. She closed her eyes and tipped her face up to the sky. Whether his being in her dreams was only her brain wanting to see him, or his spirit had truly been here, she would honor Steven's memory by living the best and fullest life she could. The past few days was long enough to remind her of the struggles to climb out of her depression the first time. Even though she was heartbroken over Nicholas and Jax, she would not go back into that dark place that had her in its grasp for too long.

And now... She had a lot to think about. Nick hadn't fought to stay with her in Oak Hollow, but *she* also had not fought for their relationship. She'd allowed fear to take over. Had she sabotaged something that could have been wonderful out of fear? A relationship was about give and take and compromise. Love took courage and work. After the harsh way she'd sent Nicholas away, he might not even answer her call, but she would start thinking about what to say to him. They owed it to one another to have a real in-depth conversation about their relationship.

Emma got up from her spot beside the trees, took a shower, ate something and started planning the best way to move forward. Priorities needed to be considered. What did she love about her life? Where was she the happiest?

Emma's Vintage & Creations by Jenny was a place that made her happy, and if they were going to venture into the online market, she was going to have to give it more focus. With Steven's life insurance money tucked away in savings, she had the funds to follow her dream. And that's why she made the decision not to go back to her teaching position in a few weeks. Not to mention, four- and five-year-olds required a lot of high energy and peppiness, and right now, she didn't have that level of pep to give.

Another reason to retire early was an inner hope that Jax would need more of her time, because she was not giving up on being part of Nick and Jax's life again. Emma gave herself permission to be happy and move on with her life while also remembering the past and the ones she'd lost

Nicholas was in the climate-controlled storage area of the auction house familiarizing himself with the newest inventory and checking pieces for any damage or need of repair. Focusing on the job at hand was a challenge because all he could do was worry about how Jax was doing with the nanny. She seemed nice enough, but she wasn't Emma. No one was.

He tested the latch on a wardrobe and examined the interior with a small flashlight from his breast pocket. An old yellowed and crumpled piece of paper was caught on the inside of the frame. Pulling it free, he saw that it was the torn page from a children's book. And if he wasn't mistaken, it was *Peter Rabbit*.

"Rabbits." Yet another thing that reminded him of Emma. Signs of her were everywhere. In a movie. A TV program she would like. A song.

The click of high heels drew his attention. "Hi, Vic. Do you need me for something?"

"No. I just needed to get up from my desk and move around. What did you find?" his sister asked.

"The page out of a children's book."

"Do you have time to talk?"

"Sure. What's up?" He folded the torn page and put it into his pocket.

"I didn't want to talk about work last night, but I think we need to. Now that Mother has basically re-tired, I think Father wants to as well, and you know how old-fashioned he is."

"All too well."

"There has always been a *male* member of the Weller family as CEO. As his only son, he is expect-ing you to take over."

"You mean now that I have passed his test and proven myself?"

She sighed and shook her head. "The way he sud-denly tossed you out of the business was a crappy thing to do."

Making sure they were alone, Nicholas lowered

his voice just in case. "Do not ever tell him this, but I'm glad he did. I've learned a lot about myself."

"You do seem different. And I imagine you'll be a different kind of CEO, and I need to know what role you see me playing."

"Actually, I want to talk to you about that, too." He carefully closed the door of the wardrobe and the latch clicked. "I plan to be a hands-on father, and I'm hoping we can share the duties here at Weller's. More like a partnership."

Her smile widened along with her blue eyes. "Really? I like the sound of that."

One of their longtime employees, Joe, walked toward them with a big smile that was definitely not directed at Nicholas. And when Nicholas glanced at his sister, she was returning the expression. *This is an interesting development.*

"Sorry to interrupt," Joe said and extended a hand to Nick. "It's good to have you back."

"Good to be back." *But is it?*

"Victoria, there is someone here to see you. He said it's about the Fuller collection that came in yesterday."

"Oh, good. I was expecting him. I'll be right there," she said and didn't take her eyes off Joe's tall broad frame as he walked away.

How had he never noticed the way they looked at one another? He'd never seen her look at her soon-to-be ex-husband like that.

"Joe is really good at his job, isn't he?" Nicholas asked.

"Yes, he is. I don't know what I would do without his help." She cleared her throat and tucked a light brown curl behind her ear. "I better go talk to this client, but I'd really like to finish this conversation later."

"Absolutely. I would, too."

When he got home that evening, he couldn't wait to hold his son. He headed straight for his suite to change out of his suit, and then he would see where the nanny had Jax. But when he got to the room he'd set up as a nursery, the new baby bed was gone. Turning in a circle, he saw that all the baby items were missing. For a brief heart-stopping moment, he had the sickening thought that it had all been a dream, and he'd awakened to his old life. Spotting a baby blanket on the floor beside the dresser, he snatched it up and brought it to his nose. The scent of his son filled his lungs. It was no dream. It was his life. Jax was his life.

Without changing his clothes, he went in search of his child, and as soon as he found him, he'd track down his mother for a much-needed chat. Apparently last night's high chair in the dining room had not been enough to bring home the point that he was in charge of his son's upbringing. Before he found

Jax, he saw his mother as he passed by the library. Inhaling a deep breath, he stopped beside her.

Control yourself until you find out what's going on.

"Hello, Nicholas. How was your day at work?"

Her eyes widened when she got a good look at his face, telling him he wasn't controlling his expression as much as he'd planned. "Where is my son?" he said in a slow, measured voice.

"In your old nursery, of course." Ice clinked in the crystal glass of whatever cocktail she was drinking. "I've spent all day having people set it up, and I have also hired a night nanny."

He pressed the palm of one hand to his forehead. "Without asking me? I had Jax set up in my suite, exactly where I want him. With me."

"Nicholas, you can't get any rest with a baby in your suite. If you want your father to announce you as his successor, you have to be at your best and show him you are serious about putting in the time and energy at work. You have to give this your full attention."

Becoming the next Weller at the helm of Weller's Auction House had been the plan his whole life. Glamorous parties and trips abroad. But now... He wanted something different. Something more fulfilling. Being a father to Jax...

And a husband to Emma.

I gave up on her too soon. I got scared and didn't

even fight for her. For us. What in the hell is wrong with me?

He'd felt the connection between them. She could not have faked all their time together. What had truly been in her head when she told him to leave?

"Son, are you listening to me?"

"No. What did you say?"

"I said, I've put his name on the lists for the best private schools."

Of course she had. "I plan to do things differently than you did, Mother."

His father entered the room. "What's all this tension?"

"A slight difference of opinion about childrearing," his mother said.

Slight? Nicholas almost laughed aloud. He couldn't get into all of this now. His mind was in too much of a spiral. "I'm going to go find my son." As he left the room, he could hear them whispering to one another.

The nanny's singing drifted from the nursery. Jax squealed and waved his arms when Nicholas entered the room, and it made the tension in his chest relax for the first time since he'd left for work. "There's my good boy."

The nanny whose name he couldn't remember held the excited baby out to him. "He sure is happy to see you. And he really has been a very good boy today."

He hugged and kissed Jax, inhaling his scent. "I'm lucky to have such a good-natured baby." He looked around the colorful room that had once been his. Memories both good and bad drifted through his mind. "What time does your shift end?"

She glanced at her watch. "In an hour."

"You can go home early today. I'll take him with me." He could see the worry on her face and knew it had to do with his mother. "Or you can stay and tidy up the room if you want."

"I think I'll do that," she said.

Now he just needed to wave off the night nanny.

Back in his bedroom, Nicholas put Jax on a blanket for tummy time. "Give me a second and then we'll play." He toed off his shiny shoes, not caring if he scuffed them, and tossed his tie on the bed. On the floor facing his son, he lay on his stomach and propped his chin on his folded hands.

Jax kicked his little legs and pushed up with his arms.

"Look how strong you're getting. My big boy is growing so fast." And as he always did, he thought how much Emma would love moments like this. He'd only spoken to Eric once since leaving Oak Hollow a few days ago, and he hadn't asked about Emma.

He'd been too stunned and hurt and embarrassed by her abrupt dismissal.

When he'd packed up and driven away from the new life he'd grown to love, he'd been numb and just trying to put one foot in front of the other and take care of his baby. Shortly after arriving in Houston, his numbness had faded, and he missed Emma with every breath. Her beautiful smile. Her laugh. And the way she sighed so sweetly when she kissed him. All he could think about was finding his way back to her. Back to the happy life they'd left behind in a small town in the Texas Hill Country.

Was she as sad as he was about being apart? Was she thinking about them just as much? "I gave up and walked away with my tail between my legs." Eye to eye with Jax, he sighed. "Your daddy is a big dummy."

Jax answered with adorable baby babble and scooted forward.

"If I had asked more questions when your mom ended things, maybe... Maybe you'd still have your mother. I wouldn't have missed your birth, and I could've been there for Aurora." He dropped his forehead onto the back of his hands. "And I've done the exact same thing with Emma. I didn't fight for our relationship. And no matter what she said, it *was* a relationship." He sat up. "And maybe it still can be. I know you love her, too."

Jax rolled over, grabbed his foot and put a big toe into his mouth.

"I don't want to miss another day with Emma. No more mistakes." He pulled his cell phone from his pocket, typed a text message to Eric and hit Send.

How is Emma?

He waited for a reply, and one came sooner than he'd expected.

She doesn't want to talk to anyone. Not even Jenny, except to tell her she was taking a week off work.

"That doesn't sound good." Panic started in the center of his chest. If she wasn't even talking to her friend and business partner, that meant she wasn't going to her shop, which was a place she loved. This meant she was as miserable as he was, and he needed to do something about it. Over the last few days, he had pictured Emma several ways: Moving on with her life and barely thinking of him. Crying her eyes out. But thinking of her in pain worried him. He sent another text.

Is she ok?

Think she has a broken heart.

"What?" He jumped to his feet. "*She's* heart-broken? Then why... Why did she send me away? And why in the hell did I go without any fight at all?" He grabbed a suitcase from his closet. "Jax, we're taking a trip back to Oak Hollow. Maybe your aunt Vic will let us borrow her Cadillac."

Jax rolled onto his tummy and cooed in agreement.

Chapter Sixteen

After their bags were packed, Nicholas knocked on the door of his sister's suite with Jax asleep on his shoulder.

"Hello, you two. What's going on?" she asked.

"Do you have time to finish our conversation about work?"

"Absolutely. Come in."

He followed her to the sitting area of her suite that was decorated in shades of ivory and blue. A color palette Emma would love. He settled onto the comfy overstuffed sofa beside her. "So, about sharing the duties—"

"Have you changed your mind about doing this together?" A frown creased her brow.

"No. Not in the way you are thinking. You should be the new chief executive." When she only stared at him with astonished eyes, he continued. "You are the oldest and you love working at the auction house. And if we are being honest, you are smarter and better at running the business than I am."

"Wow. I didn't expect you to say this. So, what role will you play?"

"I want to go back to Oak Hollow."

She smiled and held out her arms for the baby. "You're in love, aren't you?"

"I am." He eased Jax into Victoria's arms, and the baby rooted his little face against her shoulder before settling in. "But it's not just Emma who I love. I love my gallery, and the town and the way I feel when I'm there. It's the life I want for Jax."

"I'm happy for you, but I'm sad to see you and this precious little one go. I hope you'll consider keeping some connection and duties to the auction house and come in for big events."

"I like that idea. We can definitely work out some kind of agreement. And since I'm stirring everything up and making big changes, you should do the same. Go for the guy you like and don't let him get away."

"What guy?" She put a cheek on the baby's head as if to hide her expression.

"Joe. He's widowed with two young kids, right?"

"Yes. Two little girls. How did you know? We

were trying to keep it professional. Our relationship is brand-new. Only since I filed for divorce."

"Maybe I'm just more tuned into love these days. Take your little brother's advice. Fight for what makes you happy."

The next day, Nicholas and Victoria called a family meeting in the library, and they got there before their parents. Jax was playing on a blanket in front of the marble fireplace and surrounded by leather-bound volumes of classic novels on mahogany shelves with rolling ladders.

"Is this about your mother moving the baby?" his father asked as he entered the library.

"No." *At least not completely about that.* "Victoria and I want to talk to you about the future of Weller's."

"What's this about the future of Weller's?" their mother said as she joined them and took her place in the golden velvet chair beside Jax.

It surprised Nicholas when she leaned forward to hand the baby a toy and brushed her hand over his head in a tender motion. "Mother, I know you have basically retired."

"That's true."

"And I'm not far behind her," their father said.

"Nicholas and I have a plan," Victoria said. "Please hear us out."

"Victoria should be the next chief executive,"

Nicholas blurted out, eager to get this meeting over so he could head to Oak Hollow.

Franklin Weller paused with the bottle of scotch hovering over a crystal tumbler. "But it's always been a son who takes over the auction house. It's tradition. The way things have always been done."

Their mother stood abruptly and pointed a finger at her husband. "Oh, suck eggs, Franklin."

Her uncommon outburst had everyone too stunned to respond, and Nicholas and Victoria were fighting a laugh.

"Our daughter is more than capable of running Weller's, and you know it."

Their father sat down hard on the silk settee and lifted his glasses to rub his eyes. "Yes, I know Victoria is more than qualified." He looked at his daughter. "Is this what you want?"

"Yes, it is. I would be honored and excited to take the position when you are ready to retire."

Franklin looked at Nicholas. "You are ready to give up your birthright because you think you are in love with the woman in Oak Hollow?"

With perfect timing, Jax waved his arms and let out a high-pitched squeal. Victoria gave her little brother a look that translated into *keep your cool*, so Nicholas bit back the long-repressed words he wanted to say.

"Her name is Emma Blake, and she is a smart, talented business owner." He left out the part about her teaching him to be a hands-on daddy because he didn't need to rile up his father any more than he already was. "And I don't *think* I love her, I know I do. I also love the business I've started there. But I would like to continue to be part of the family business in some capacity. Just not full-time. And not as CEO."

"I see," Franklin said. "Tell me more about your plan."

They talked, and thankfully their father listened and accepted their ideas. Once everything was worked out, Nicholas and Jax were on the road in his sister's safe car. Announcing his feelings to his family had made him more than sure about his decision. He was in love with Emma and wanted to spend the rest of his life with her. And God willing, she would want the same thing once he assured her that he would wait until she was ready and not push her. He would get his own place so she didn't feel crowded or pressured. He'd romance her and give her the time and love she deserved.

Even if she sent him away a second time, at least he'd know he'd tried. If he didn't, he'd always wonder and never forgive himself for giving up. She needed to know he wanted to spend his life with her and have her be a mother to his son. Not because his son needed a mom but because they wanted *her* in their lives. He would do his best to convince her how good they were together.

* * *

After a phone call from Jenny, Emma started her car and drove to the town square. It was out of character for her partner to forget to lock the door of their shop, but mistakes happened. Since the businesses were closed, she got a parking spot right in front of her shop and was even more confused to see the light on, too. This wasn't like Jenny at all. She went inside and stopped short. On the floor in front of the register, Jax was in his car seat, and when he saw her, he kicked his little legs and squealed.

"Oh, my sweet baby." She rushed to him, tears already trickling down her face, and unbuckled him from the seat. She hadn't known if she would ever see him again. "I've missed you so, so much." She squeezed him tight and dropped kisses all over him. "Where is your daddy?"

"At last," Nicholas stepped out from behind a clothing rack, singing a few lines of the song that had come to mean something to them.

Her pulse kicked up another notch, and she smiled through her tears. She held the baby closer and listened to his deep voice until he stopped in front of her. "What are you doing here? I thought you went home."

"Home is wherever you are, Em."

A sob caught in her throat. She was afraid to believe this was real. Afraid she'd wake up at any moment and discover she was dreaming.

"You asked me to leave, but I shouldn't have gone." He moved a step closer. "I should've stayed and fought for our relationship."

"You're serious?" Her heart was beating so fast she was trembling. "What about Weller's?"

"My sister is taking over as CEO, and I'm working on a part-time basis. My focus will be my gallery and building a life here in Oak Hollow."

"Really? You're sure about this?"

"Positive. It's no secret that you love my son. I know I'm speaking for an infant, but as his daddy, I have it on good authority that he loves you and wants you in his life just as much as I do." He took a long slow breath. "I'm praying that you might extend that love to me as well. Because I'm so in love with you, my beautiful, sweet Em."

Happiness rushed through her. She accepted his outstretched hand and let him hold her with the baby between them. "I love Jax, and I love you, for you. Not just because you're his father. You are worthy of love all on your own." She caressed his cheek, stubbled as if he hadn't taken the time to shave in his rush to get to her.

"I have a new deal I'd like to run by you."

"I'm listening."

"We started with one week of baby lessons for me doing some manual labor. I definitely got the better end of that deal, and I still owe you big-time for turning me into a responsible parent."

"Nick, you have always been better than you realize."

"At whatever pace you are comfortable with, will you consider creating a life with us? You, me and Jax. Day by day. Year by year. Birthdays and Christmases. I'm only asking for one thing. Instead of one week, I want one lifetime, together. As a family."

She gasped and looked between her two loves. "You want me to be his mother?"

"My sweet Em, you *are* his mother. But I know you need time. We will get our own place and we can take things as slow as you need to. I won't rush you again."

Jax grabbed two handfuls of her hair and gummed her chin, making her laugh.

"If you get one lifetime, then I want you both to come back home to the house where we started our relationship. I want you to plant trees with me every year, and we need to add a third tree. Together we need to plant a tree for Aurora as well as Steven and Rose, so Jax will know where he comes from. So he will know his whole family tree."

Nick wiped a tear from the corner of his eye. "That is a wonderful idea, and I agree one hundred percent."

Her smile bloomed and she could feel happiness and love in every cell of her body. "What do you say, Jax? Do you want to be a family?"

The baby blew a raspberry and held on to both of them, making their laughs mix with a few tears, and a whole lot of love.

Epilogue

The summer day was bright and clear, and Jax toddled around the backyard playing with his new puppy. Emma and Nicholas had just finished planting the third tree. Along with another red oak for Steven and a pink blooming crepe myrtle for Rose, this one was a peach tree in remembrance of Aurora. She had chosen this tree so someday Jax could pick the fruit and they could make pies as they told him stories about his birth mother.

Nicholas wrapped his arms around his wife and cradled the baby bump that was just beginning to show. "How are you feeling, honey?"

Turning with happiness shining in her eyes, she kissed him. "Wonderful. I love you so much."

"I love you, too."

"Mama," Jax called to her and giggled as the puppy licked his toes.

They went to their son and scooped him up into a hug between them. "Are you having fun, my sweet boy?" she asked him. Her answer was a wet kiss on her cheek.

A car pulled slowly down the driveway, and they waved to Marco as he got out.

"Look who is here to see you," Nick said to his son.

Jax wiggled to get down and then eagerly ran to his uncle for a hugged.

They all enjoyed the rest of the beautiful afternoon playing as a family beside a row of special trees.

* * * * *

Don't miss these other great single dad romances:

A Double Dose of Happiness
By Teri Wilson

A Starlight Summer
By Michelle Major

The Triplet's Secret Wish
By Cathy Gillen Thacker

Available now from Harlequin Special Edition!

#2929 ONE NIGHT WITH THE MAVERICK

Montana Mavericks: Brothers & Broncos • by Melissa Senate

Everyone thinks Shari Lormand and veterinarian Felix Sanchez are a couple. Unfortunately, the guarded widower has made it abundantly clear all he's looking for is a buddy. Shari is afraid she's hurtling toward another heartbreak. But with a little help from the town psychic, she and Felix just might have a shot after all...

#2930 FOREVER, PLUS ONE

Holliday, Oregon • by Wendy Warren

Nikki Choi loves the boisterous family she was adopted into as a baby. But dreams of her own happy-ever-after are dashed when her fiancé suddenly calls off the wedding. Leave it to her BFF Evan Northrup to come to her rescue. But the single dad seems intent on keeping things pretend, while Nikki is shocked to be falling wildly, deeply for her old friend...

#2931 THE DESIGNER'S SECRET

Small Town Secrets • by Nina Crespo

Usually sensible Layla Price stuns herself when she spends the night with a handsome stranger. Blaming it on a freak rainstorm and Bastian Raynes's heroic rescue, Layla believes she'll never see him again. She's only in this small town to end some silly family feud. Except...Bastian's family is on the other end of that feud and Layla's hiding her real identity!

#2932 THE SPIRIT OF SECOND CHANCES

Heart & Soul • by Synithia Williams

Single mom Cierra Greene is determined to succeed in real estate. Too bad her most lucrative property for sale is...haunted? Reluctantly, she seeks out Wesley Livingston, a cohost of a popular paranormal investigation show, for help. Cierra and Wesley try to ignore their unfinished business, but when old feelings resurface, things get complicated...

#2933 A CHARMING CHRISTMAS ARRANGEMENT

Charming, Texas • by Heatherly Bell

Stacy Hartsell thought finding her unborn baby's father was going to be the hard part. Except widowed ex-SEAL Adam Cruz is determined to step up—and his argument that his veteran health care is better than her freelancer plan is a fairly convincing one. Giving in to their feelings *could* put their convenient arrangement in jeopardy...or lead to a second chance to find lasting love this Christmas!

#2934 CINDERELLA'S LAST STAND

Seven Brides for Seven Brothers • by Michelle Lindo-Rice

Despite crushing on his Prince Charming looks, personal assistant Maddie Henry has had enough of Axel Harrington not recognizing her value. Well, this Cinderella is shattering the glass slipper to pursue her dream career! The "Sexiest Man Alive" has two weeks to find a new assistant. And to realize that Maddie is the key to his happily-ever-after.

Cierra's lips lifted in a smile that brightened his dark
corner of the coffee shop as she straightened. "Oh, good,
you remember me," she said, as if he could possibly
forget her.

How could he forget Cierra Greene? Head cheerleader,
class president, most popular girl in school and slayer of
teenage boys' hearts.

"Yeah…I remember you." He managed to keep his
voice calm even though his heart thumped as if he'd had
a dozen cappuccinos.

"I was worried because you didn't return any of my
calls." She tilted her head to the side and her thick, dark
hair shifted. Her smile didn't go away, but there was the
barest hint of accusation in her voice.

Wesley shifted in his seat. He hadn't returned her
calls because ever since the day Cierra told him after a

basketball game that she was ditching him for his former best friend, he'd vowed to never speak to her again. He realized vows made in high school didn't have to follow him into adulthood, but the moment he'd heard her voice message saying she'd like to meet up and talk, he'd deleted it and tried to move on with his life.

"I've been busy," he said.

"Good thing I caught you here, then, huh?" She moved to the opposite side of the table and pulled out the other chair and sat.

"How did you know I was here?"

"Mrs. Montgomery," she said, as if he should have known that one of the most respected women in town would give his whereabouts to her. She must have read the confusion on his face because she laughed, that lighthearted laugh that, unfortunately, still made his heart skip a beat. "When I couldn't reach you, my mom called around. Mrs. Montgomery said you typically spend Friday afternoons here. So, here I am!" She held out her arms and spoke as if she were a present.

Her bright smile and enthusiasm stunned him for a second. Wesley cleared his throat and took a sip of his coffee to compose himself. How many years later—fifteen—and he still had the lingering remnants of a crush on her?

Come on, Wes, you gotta do better than that!

He took a long breath and looked back at her. "Here you are."

Get 4 FREE REWARDS!

We'll send you 2 FREE Books plus 2 FREE Mystery Gifts.

FREE Value Over **$20**

Both the **Harlequin® Special Edition** and **Harlequin® Heartwarming™** series feature compelling novels filled with stories of love and strength where the bonds of friendship, family and community unite.

YES! Please send me 2 FREE novels from the Harlequin Special Edition or Harlequin Heartwarming series and my 2 FREE gifts (gifts are worth about $10 retail). After receiving them, if I don't wish to receive any more books, I can return the shipping statement marked "cancel." If I don't cancel, I will receive 6 brand-new Harlequin Special Edition books every month and be billed just $5.24 each in the U.S. or $5.99 each in Canada, a savings of at least 13% off the cover price or 4 brand-new Harlequin Heartwarming Larger-Print books every month and be billed just $5.99 each in the U.S. or $6.49 each in Canada, a savings of at least 20% off the cover price. It's quite a bargain! Shipping and handling is just 50¢ per book in the U.S. and $1.25 per book in Canada.* I understand that accepting the 2 free books and gifts places me under no obligation to buy anything. I can always return a shipment and cancel at any time by calling the number below. The free books and gifts are mine to keep no matter what I decide.

Choose one: ☐ **Harlequin Special Edition** ☐ **Harlequin Heartwarming**
(235/335 HDN GRCQ)   **Larger-Print**
(161/361 HDN GRC3)

Name (please print)

Address   Apt. #

City   State/Province   Zip/Postal Code

Email: Please check this box ☐ if you would like to receive newsletters and promotional emails from Harlequin Enterprises ULC and its affiliates. You can unsubscribe anytime.

Mail to the Harlequin Reader Service:
IN U.S.A.: P.O. Box 1341, Buffalo, NY 14240-8531
IN CANADA: P.O. Box 603, Fort Erie, Ontario L2A 5X3

Want to try 2 free books from another series? Call 1-800-873-8635 or visit www.ReaderService.com.

*Terms and prices subject to change without notice. Prices do not include sales taxes, which will be charged (if applicable) based on your state or country of residence. Canadian residents will be charged applicable taxes. Offer not valid in Quebec. This offer is limited to one order per household. Books received may not be as shown. Not valid for current subscribers to the Harlequin Special Edition or Harlequin Heartwarming series. All orders subject to approval. Credit or debit balances in a customer's account(s) may be offset by any other outstanding balance owed by or to the customer. Please allow 4 to 6 weeks for delivery. Offer available while quantities last.

Your Privacy—Your information is being collected by Harlequin Enterprises ULC, operating as Harlequin Reader Service. For a complete summary of the information we collect, how we use this information and to whom it is disclosed, please visit our privacy notice located at corporate.harlequin.com/privacy-notice. From time to time we may also exchange your personal information with reputable third parties. If you wish to opt out of this sharing of your personal information, please visit readerservice.com/consumerschoice or call 1-800-873-8635. **Notice to California Residents**—Under California law, you have specific rights to control and access your data. For more information on these rights and how to exercise them, visit corporate.harlequin.com/california-privacy.

HSEHW22R2

HARLEQUIN
PLUS

Announcing a **BRAND-NEW** multimedia subscription service for romance fans like you!

Read, Watch and Play.

Experience the easiest way to get the romance content you crave.

Start your **FREE 7 DAY TRIAL** at <u>www.harlequinplus.com/freetrial</u>.